The Weekend That Ch;

Chapter 1

It was a bright beautiful Friday, and the work week came to an end. That late afternoon sky was simply perfect with the right amount of sun, coupled with just a handful of stark white clouds, that were sporadically spread apart. There was a soft, gentle breeze that made anyone with a convertible feel like they were on top of the world.

That's the way Caleb felt right now. The wind was blowing through his spiky blonde hair as he felt like a million bucks in his moderately priced, 7-year-old, convertible. Finally, the weekend is here and it's time to decompress from his stressful job as a computer programmer/analyst. He was now heading home to a cute house he rented in a quiet, upscale neighborhood.

Caleb's cells phone rings. He glances on the display and notices it's his friend, Christian. He quickly hits the button to put it on speaker mode.

"Hey Chris, what's up?"

"Congrats bro'!... I got your text. That's a great promotion. Let's celebrate this weekend. I have a bunch of things going on with Marissa, but Sunday night is free. I can get everyone together and we'll meet at the sports bar," Christian replied, "Marissa has a couple friends that know who are and were asking all about you."

"Haha..." Caleb chucked, "just what I need... more crazy college girls to mess up my head and cause a distraction."

Christian replies, "That's what you get for being so good-looking."

"Yeah, yeah… okay, Sunday night is great. I'll see ya' then," Caleb confirmed, then ended the call.

The brilliant 22-year-old landed an intern position with amazing pay, working for a high-profile, fortune 500 company six months ago. His skill set and his dedicated work ethic have paid off, making upper management really take notice of him. So much so, that today, he was offered a full-time opportunity and a promotion from the entry level programmer position. This new promotion comes with quite a pay increase that makes him smile from ear to ear just thinking about it. Simply put, it's a lot of money, especially for someone who exited college early and still hasn't finished getting a bachelor's degree.

Even with all this great news, this isn't Caleb's dream job. Ever since he was little, playing with his Lego and Matchbox toys, he wanted to be a police officer. Sure, he would miss the high-paying salary that he's got a taste of, but he would definitely leave the corporate world of suits and ties in a heartbeat, if he was accepted into the police academy. The fact is, the entry-level position he was in was a great paying job, with a nice career path. Working for a large company and making that kind of money right out of school is just about every student's dream... and he didn't even finish college!

That entry-level job alone allowed him to rent a small but beautiful home on a quiet dead-end street in the suburbs. So now, with an even higher new pay scale, and a definite career path, purchasing a home like this would well be within his reach. One thing for sure is that he loves coming home every day to the quiet, upscale neighborhood that borders a nature preserve.

The quaint home has stone walls separating the woods behind it and is located at the end of a cul-de-sac. It's on an acre of land with only 1 house to the left. That house is big and beautiful, boasting a contemporary flare. His neighbors, the Doyle's, are just as nice as their house is. James and Megan Doyle seem to be in their mid to upper 40's and are at least twice his age. Regardless, they are super friendly, and overall just amazing people.

Jim, Mr. Doyle is a really cool, laid back kind of guy. He's a Pharmacist but you would never know that with his hippy vibe and style. When he's home, it seems like he's always landscaping, fixing things, and tinkering with his cars. Mr. Doyle has a certain way about himself and he always makes Caleb laugh when they talk.

Mrs. Doyle is an APRN and literally one step away from being a doctor. She's a loving and nurturing mom that now mostly works from home doing tele-medicine and substitute teaching. She is completely different from her husband. She's kind of plain but very pretty in her own simple, woman next door, kind of way. Unlike her husband, Mrs. Doyle remains active and enjoys playing tennis, pickle ball, yoga, and bike riding. She would be the first to tell you that she would like to lose 5 or 10 pounds and needs to stop baking cakes and cookies. However, many of her friends compliment the way she fills out her clothing and the way she plays and excels at sports.

The cool couple has 2 teenage sons, Ryder 19, and Dillon 15. Ryder is one of Caleb's really close friends. They both attended the same high school and played on the football team together. Ryder isn't home much since he's enjoying his first year at college and the freedom of living on campus. It's about an hour away from home but still convenient enough for him to pop in a few times a month for his mom's cooking. Today must be one of those days. Ryder's car is in the driveway next door and Caleb is looking forward to seeing him and catching up. The two of them still have a lot in common and always capture attention with their natural good looks and athletic physiques. There's never a shortage of girls vying for them when they hangout together.

The Doyle's youngest son, Dillon, is the typical 15, almost 16-year old. He's a wise ass, pesky little nuisance that is always trying to act cool. He's constantly hanging off his brother's shoulders and often wanders into Caleb's garage when he's exercising and lifting weights. Of course, Caleb finds it amusing but also annoying to watch Dillon attempt to pick up heavy weights that are way beyond his capacity. He's constantly stopping his own workout to make sure he doesn't actually hurt himself.

As Caleb pulls into his driveway and exits his car. He presses a button to automatically open his garage door. The smile on his face says it all as he relishes his home gym complete with a matted floor, various benches, equipment, weights and mirrors. He felt this was a much better use for his garage than just parking his car, especially since it overlooks his beautiful back yard. He waved to Mr. Doyle, who is at it again on his John Deere lawn mower, perfectly grooming his yard. Ryder waves and then walks over as he sees Caleb in the driveway.

"Caleb, what's up bud?"
"You looking good dude, really buff!" He looks his friend up and down dressed to the nine in business attire, that still manages to show off his killer body.
"This is much different than our football uniforms," Ryder laughs, "How are you?"

Caleb gives him the brotherly hug and replies, "Hey bro', good to see ya'... Yeah, I'm good... tired, but really good. The job is challenging but very rewarding." "Today they offered me a full-time position."

"Wow! Congratulations, I'm proud of you buddy!" Ryder replies.

"How are you? How's college? Are you home for the weekend?" Caleb asks.

"It's awesome! And yes, I'm going upstate, camping with my dad and my snot nose little brother. My mom's staying home. The woods, fishing, campfires, just isn't her thing." He laughs.

Mrs. Doyle steps onto her back porch, waves, and calls out.

"Hi Caleb... Hey Ryder, did you see your brother?"
"He was supposed to have all his homework and chores done and also have the table set for dinner. You guys are going away all weekend and he needs to get them done."

Her frustrated look is obvious as she tries calling him, "He's not answering his phone and he's not responding to my text. I'm starting to get worried."

Caleb chimes in to put her at ease, "I saw him on my way home, Mrs. Doyle. I even waved to him. He's playing basketball in the park."

Ryder responds, "I'll ride my bike and tell him to come home, Mom," he turns to Caleb, "You up for a bike ride, Caleb?"

Caleb replies, "Sure, let me go change my clothes. I was going to work-out in the garage anyway."

"Cool, let's workout together after we ride and tell my dumb-ass brother to get home." Ryder suggests.

"Hey Mom, I'm going to workout with Caleb since we don't get to hang out that much. Don't count on me for dinner," Ryder tells her.

Mrs. Doyle responds, "Sure honey, I'll put a plate aside for you, and one for you also, Caleb." Her tone suddenly changes, "Make sure you tell your brother to call me and to get his butt home immediately!"

Caleb thanks her as he goes inside to change into his exercise clothes. Moments later, him and Ryder ride their bikes to the park. Ryder waves as he spots his brother Dillon on the basketball court. Dillon just about ignores him and is acting all cool talking with two girls. He tells him to call their mom and return home immediately to get his chores done. Of course, Dillon shrugs it off, remains on the court, and continues to act like mister big shot in front of the two cute, young schoolgirls.

Ryder and Caleb ride their bikes back and proceed to workout in Caleb's garage. Ryder lets his mom know that he absolutely gave Dillon the message to get home and do his chores. They leave the garage door open, turn up the music, and proceed to go through a strenuous workout.

Slightly over an hour has gone by and there's still no sign of Dillon. Mrs. Doyle, feeling a combination of frustration and concern, walks over and enters Caleb's garage. With the music blasting, and their backs turned away from the door, they didn't know that Mrs. Doyle had entered the garage. She takes a moment and is careful not to interrupt them in the middle of an exercise. Caleb, is doing a set of squats with an impressive amount of weight, as her son, Ryder, is closely spotting him.

Mrs. Doyle gets momentarily flustered at the site of Caleb's muscles popping out of that faded, powder-blue, tank top he's wearing. She also didn't mind having to wait, as her big blue eyes were totally focused like a laser beam on his more than cute, tight, round ass. She definitely felt a little tingle throughout her body as she watched Caleb squat low and then return upward, tightly squeezing his glutes together, at the completion of each rep. She must have timed it perfectly, and caught him when he just started, because she was more than happy to take the sight of him doing at least 8 to 10 rep of that butt clenching exercise.

Being a nurse for 20 years, and seeing more than her share of bodies, Mrs. Doyle, has always been an admirer of a nice rear-end. Only one of her really close friends, Marcy Beck, knows this sexy obsession of hers. In fact, they both laugh about being total ass-lovers and having this in common. It's a guarantee that seeing a hot, athletic guy, with an amazing ass, will always make one of them whisper a comment to each other. Megan usually beats Marcy to the punch and always mentions what she would do with the guy's ass, if she was ever fortunate enough to get her hands on it. Of course, the two silly moms usually fantasize, tease, and joke to each other that they could both double team the hot jock and share in the fun.

Even though it's always a comical comment and conversation, it definitely reveals some hidden kinks about Megan Doyle, and Marcy as well. There's definitely another whole side to both of them that's just dying to come out of hibernation. In fact, they purposely make it a habit to meet at a cute little coffee shop right next to the college campus. It's not the coffee that makes them go there a couple times a week, it's the sight of the hot college athletes coming in and out for their caffeine fix.

Right now, it's safe to say, that she's definitely distracted by Caleb's athletic hiney which looks like a basketball that she would love to dribble. Once Mrs. Doyle regains her composure, she asks her son, "Ry, Where the heck is Dillon?… Did you tell him I wanted him home immediately?"

Ryder immediately responds, "Yep, I told him Mom, but he was acting all cool in front of the girls and he flat-out ignored me."

Mrs. Doyle's face turned beet red as she replied, "Oh, he did? That's it!… I'll go get him myself!"

Ryder chuckles, "Try not to embarrass him too much mom. He's just being an idiot and trying to act like he's all it in front of the girls."

"Well, it's up to him. I'll give him the chance not to embarrass himself in public, but when I get him home alone, that's another story!"

Ryder chuckles and turns to Caleb, "Oh Shit, he's really in trouble now!". They both watch as Mrs. Doyle hastily walks back to her home to retrieve her car keys.

Caleb's eyes opened wide as he's never seen that angry side of Mrs. Doyle before. She's always happy, smiling, baking cookies, cakes, and pies. This is an entirely different side to her. He comments to Ryder, "Wow, I never seen your mom angry. Especially, not like that."

Ryder replies, "It doesn't happen often and it really takes a lot to set her off. She has a lot of patience and always gives us a chance to do the right thing. Dillon is clearly misbehaving, and not listening. Plus, to make matters worse, he's totally disrespecting her," He concludes with a slight chuckle, "Trust me, I know all too well what's about to go down!"

"Won't your dad just go get him?" Caleb asked.

Ryder flat out laughs, "Haha, my dad? No, he's way too easy going. Once in a while he'll ground us, but that's about it. My mom is a real take-charge lady, she handles everything else... And I mean... everything!"

Just then, Dillon comes through the wooded trail riding his bike. He completely bypasses his own house, and continues to ride his bike down Caleb's driveway. He gets off it, leaves it right there in the driveway, and walks straight into the garage. He immediately interrupts their workout and starts picking up weights and screwing around on the equipment. Once again, he acts all cool and tries to curl and lift more than his body can handle. Ryder looks at him and makes it clear that he's in trouble.

"Dude, mom is really mad. She went inside to get her car keys, and you know what else... She planned on driving to the park to get you. You better get in the house and get your shit done."

Mrs. Doyle is just about to get into her car when she spots Dillon's bike in Caleb's driveway. She quietly closes her car door and heads over to Caleb's garage. As she approaches, she easily hears every word of the conversation.

"Dude, I'm serious. Stop trying to act all cool. Go get your chores and homework done. We're going away for the whole weekend with dad... Don't ruin the fun," Ryder tells him.

Dillon reacts to his brother, "Chill out you sissy. It's no big deal. Mom's probably busy cooking up a storm and getting food ready for our camping trip. I'll get my chores done tonight and my homework... I don't know... at some time... whenever. Stop being a bossy dick head. We all know that you're such a pussy... Such a mommy's boy."

Ryder quickly responds, "Dude, you better chill. I'm about 2 seconds from knocking you out!"

Dillon continues to provoke him, "Oooh, I'm so scared." He sarcastically replies.

"Fucking pussy… you think you're so cool now Mr. College stud."
"You're not cool, you're still my asshole big brother."

Mrs. Doyle hears every word and is absolutely furious at Dillon's behavior as she makes a bee-line straight to Caleb's garage.

Chapter 2

Caleb watches as his attractive neighbor, Mrs. Doyle enters his garage in a complete huff. It's clear that she's mad at hell at her son Dillon. Even though she has this furrowed look between her eyebrows and has her lips tightly pursed, with a face that shows she means business, Caleb can't help but take notice of how beautiful she looks.

Plus, Mrs. Doyle isn't just wearing a nice outfit, she's absolutely rocking a super-thin, super-pretty, red and white patterned sundress that's hugging all of her curves in more than the right way. Those wide, beautiful hips of hers are framing her round, slightly chunky, pumpkin-shaped, rear-end so perfectly, that it's literally causing that one main part of Caleb's lower body to pulsate with excitement.

His attention then goes to her piercing blue eyes that are half squinting with a stern, fierce look. It's definitely a look that Caleb's never even come close to seeing from her before. Up to this point, he'd always seen his friend's mom joyful, loving, and totally easy going. There's no doubt that Caleb always thought Mrs. Doyle was a pretty lady. On occasion, he would even joke and harass his friend Ryder, telling him that his mom was hot. It was always in good fun and both of them would continue to crack and edge each other on.

Mrs. Doyle has always looked nice, even when she's just wearing a pair of baggy sweats, leggings, or jeans. That's what she would usually wear as she's doing things around the house or tending to her beautiful flowers outside. After all, this is his good friend's mom, his next door neighbor, who's house constantly smells amazing from everything she makes. Then more times than not, she would knock on Caleb's door, sending him a plate of whatever deliciousness she made. That tender, loving, side of Mrs. Doyle, is such a huge contrast to the stern, fierce-looking woman that he's seeing now. The way she looks, coupled with her current mood and mannerism right now in his garage, has Caleb totally stunned and equally excited.

Caleb's eyes open even wider now and his head snaps back a bit in shock, as he becomes aware that Mrs. Doyle is clenching the thick, leather strap tightly in her right hand. Ryder looks at his mom ready to use the strap, and then looks over at his brother Dillon. Ryder shook his head in total disbelief. He couldn't even fathom how foolishly his younger brother acted, and why. They both know perfectly well what happens when they misbehave, or even worse, blatantly disrespect their mom.

Unfortunately, Dillon was much more interested in acting cool in front of the girls than heeding Ryder's warnings about returning home and finishing his chores. Ryder smirks as he knows exactly what his mom is about to do to his younger brother. Caleb's eyes remained glued to Mrs. Doyle as he watches her approach Dillon. She glares intently at him and then taps the strap on the palm of her left hand.

"You! That language! Get your rear-end home. You are in for it mister!" She scolds and shoots Dillon a super-stern look that he knows all too well.

Dillon's eyes light up like the sun as he sees the thick leather strap clenched tightly in his mom's right hand.

"Okay! Okay mom!" is all he can muster as he hesitates and foolishly backs as far away from her as possible, retreating to the opposite side of the garage.

He still hesitates, and in a frozen type of manner, extends both of his hands upward, in a "wait, hold on" kind-of-way. The look in his mom's eyes confirmed that she was now more than ready to go to town on that rear-end of his.

"I told you to get your butt home!" Her patience is now completely gone.

Mrs. Doyle quickly jogs over and pursues him with the strap. Dillon is trapped and he backed himself into a corner, as he watches his mom hastily approach him. He nervously pleads, "No… Please, I'm sorry Mom. I'm going, I'm going… I'll get my chores done."

Mrs. Doyle's patience has expired way past her breaking point and she simply isn't having it. She wastes no time and once Dillon is within reach, she forcefully grabs his left arm and spins him around. She raises the leather strap and swings it hard with a fast, fluid motion. The sound resonates with plenty of reverb throughout Caleb's garage as it connects over Dillon's thin shorts. Dillon's feet actually come off the ground, and he yelps in pain, "Yeoow!"

In a natural reaction, Dillon spins his body away from her, and immediately moves his right hand over his butt. He clenches it tightly, tucking his body inward as a response to the pain. His mom is still holding onto his left-arm like a vice-grip. She displays her strength and forcefully spins him back around, with his rear-end facing out.

She quickly and smartly uses her body weight to pin Dillon into the corner of the garage. Without wasting another second, she grabs the waistband of his shorts together with his underwear and aggressively tugs them down to his knees. It's very clear, that this definitely isn't Mrs. Doyle's first rodeo. The way she handles Dillon, and the wear and tear that's evident on that thick leather strap, confirms that she obviously has plenty of experience with disciplining her boys.

Caleb is shell shocked and gets an eyeful as he watches Dillon become fully exposed by his mom. His eyes are now totally glued and fixated on Mrs. Doyle, and the way she's handling her bratty son. He notices how intently her eyes are focused, like a laser beam, on Dillon's bare bottom as she keeps a tight hold onto his left arm. Mrs. Doyle bends her torso, causing her plump booty to stick out even further as she raises the leather strap high in the air. Of course, Caleb's eyes now focus on the amazing sight of her beautiful, overly round, butt arching out underneath that pretty sundress, as she delivers the strap to Dillon's bare bottom.

Mrs. Doyle delivers a relentless swat that instantly paints a red stripe dead in the center of Dillon's stark white bottom. He lets out a cry and again hops in pain. His private parts bounce up and down as his entire lower body is in full view to his brother and Caleb. As his mom maintains a firm hold on his left arm, he tries to move his right hand from trying to cover his bottom, to trying to cover his genitals. His mom reacts quickly and takes full advantage of having a totally clear path to his bare bottom. Without wasting another second, she swings the strap and adds another bright red stripe to his rear-end.

"Oooow! Please Mom!" He cries out as his hand moves from covering his genitals back to trying to cover his bottom.

Mrs. Doyle doesn't let go of his left arm and starts marching him out of Caleb's garage and back in the direction of their house. Dillon waddles like a penguin and does all he can to keep up, as he's being pulled by his mom. He manages to pull up his underwear up, causing his mom to scold and remind him, "Go ahead you can pull them up now, but once I get you inside, I'm pulling them right back down!" She relays to him, "I'm not done with your hiney! Now march, mister!"

As Caleb watches the action, Ryder continues to shake his head in disbelief. He still has no idea why his brother decided to act so stupid. He knows how stern their mom is and for him to not take her warnings seriously was just asinine. Once Dillon manages to pull his shorts up, he literally runs out of Caleb's garage and toward his house.

Mrs. Doyle now turns to Caleb and Ryder, "I'm so sorry that I had to interrupt your workout." She says to them. Her attention then turns to Ryder, "And Ryder, I'm really proud of you for not punching your brother out for the names he called you."

"No sweat mom, he was just being stupid and trying to act all cool." Ryder replies.

"Well, I gave him a fair chance and for him to display that type of behavior is unacceptable. You know what happens when you guys blatantly misbehave and totally disrespect me."

"Yes, you gave him a fair chance, Mom." Ryder confirms, "I told him to call you and come home. He absolutely ignored it and deserved it."

"Well, that hiney of his is gonna get a few more of my strap. Then I'm gonna deal with that foul language. His mouth is in for a good dose of soap as well!" She added in a stern tone.

Once again, Caleb's eyes widely open when he hears and sees this totally different side of Mrs. Doyle. Her tone and sternness is such a vast contrast to the sweet, loving neighbor that's always a ray of sunshine. He feels all his manhood as he becomes totally erect, realizing how turned on he got watching her discipline her son.

The way she pursued her bratty son grabbed him, pulled down his shorts, and administered the strap to his bare bottom is something Caleb will never forget. Right now, his eyes can't help but follow her every step as she exits his garage. The way her hips swayed making her butt shake from side to side under that thin sundress, made his erection even more intense. He watches as she walks with a purpose at a much faster pace than normal back to her home. The thick, leather strap is still firmly clenched in her right hand as she swings the door open to her home and disappears from his view.

Ryder turns to him and jokes, "Yep, those tennis lessons really paid off for my mom. She's swinging with such accuracy and force these days."

His joke breaks the tension of the situation and makes Caleb laugh out loud. Ryder continues, "I'll head home and shower, then I'll bring the food over and we'll eat out on the deck."

Chapter 3

Caleb nods and Ryder walks back to his house. His mind is completely blown, to say the least. He has even more respect for his older neighbor and her ability to lay down the law with her kids. Of course, that's not all he's feeling right now for Mrs. Doyle. Like a light switch, something totally turned on within him. His view of Ryder's mom, the usually cool, plain, woman next door, had suddenly changed. Just like that, Caleb is now infatuated and drawn to her beyond belief. His mind is creating every image of how she must be disciplining Dillon behind closed doors.

Caleb heads off to his bathroom, strips down, and gets into the shower. He quickly lathers soap all over his body as his hand starts rapidly stroking himself. He closes his eyes and fantasizes about getting aggressively handled like that by Mrs. Doyle. He now creates a video in his mind of her pulling his pants down and going to town on him with that thick leather strap of hers.

The vulnerability and the embarrassment of having his neighbor and good friend's mom see him naked, and redden his butt, is priming his penis to erupt like a volcano. It doesn't take long at all and within minutes, Caleb's moans as he ejaculates to a much needed release. He takes a few additional minutes to soak his head underneath the semi-warm water of the shower, before drying himself off and getting into clean clothes. Now with a clear head, he meets Ryder outside on the deck overlooking his beautiful backyard.

"Dude, your mom is fierce!" he relays to Ryder, "I had no idea she had that in her."

Ryder laughs, "Oh yeah, when she gets to that point... Look out!" He continues, "Last month she found out that I was drinking at school. When I came home, she gave me an option. I could take a good old fashion strapping from her or get my car taken away and move back home. Needless to say, I took the strapping."

Caleb's interest is totally peaked as he responds and pries for more information. "Wow! She still spanks you? How? Where? Bare?"

"She had me bend over the arm of the sofa in our family room. And yes... bare ass!" He responds with a slight tremble of embarrassment in his voice.

He quickly chimes in, "Caleb, don't get the wrong idea. My mom is the most amazing, loving woman on this planet. One thing I have to say is that she always gives us a warning and she's totally fair. It's only when we disrespect her and behave so badly that she disciplines us like that."

Caleb nods his head in agreement and listens as Ryder continues, "Then a short while later, after she spanks us, she'll sit down with us to calmly talk about it. She'll explain her actions and the reason why she spanked us. My mom really gives us the world and does everything for me and Dillon. It's just that she won't tolerate any bullshit, and for that, I respect her so much."

Caleb asks, "Did she ever discipline you like that? In front of someone? I mean… fully exposed?"

Ryder thinks for a moment and then responds, "Only once a few years ago. I called Mrs. Beck up the street a bitch because she yelled at me. It was my fault and my mom warned me not to play baseball too close to any houses. I didn't listen and I hit the ball through Mrs. Beck's window."

His nervous chuckle makes Caleb laugh also. Caleb's ears were itching to hear more of the details. He waits a bit to see if Ryder elaborates and tells him more about what happened that day. He really wanted to hear how his mom disciplined him. Unable to wait any longer, he pries, "So, then what?"

"Mrs. Beck walked over to my house and told my mom." Ryder continues to tell the story.

"My mom called me inside. She grabbed the strap and the wooden spoon and waited for me at the door with Mrs. Beck. I knew I was in trouble and the moment I stepped into my house, my mom got down to business on my butt!" Ryder continues.

"She quickly yanked my jeans and underwear down, then pulled them completely off my body along with my sneakers. She grabbed my earlobe and marched me to the couch, giving me several swats with the wooden spoon along the way. I was fully exposed as Mrs. Beck stood there and saw everything, and I mean EVERYTHING! I was dancing from leg to leg just like Dillon was. I still remember the smirk on Mrs. Beck's face as she looked at my penis bouncing up and down, and my mom reddening my ass."

"Man Ryder, you must have been totally embarrassed," Caleb replies.

"More then you can ever imagine bro', and that was just the beginning of my spanking that day. My mom marched me to the sofa in the living room. She made me lay down on my back and lifted my legs up. She paddled me so hard with that wooden spoon… it broke! All the while, Mrs. Beck stood over and watched."

"WOW! Holy Shit Ryder!" Caleb blurts out as his mind is busy creating the images to match Ryder's story.

Ryder gives him the last few details, "After she broke the wooden spoon, she turned me over on my stomach and gave me several with the leather strap. I was howling!"

Caleb replies, "Oh man!"

"Just when I thought it was over, she pulled me up and held me over the couch and she handed the strap to Mrs. Beck. Needless to say, I got several from Mrs. Beck as well." Ryder concludes.

"No way! Mrs. Beck also strapped you? Kailee's Mom?" Caleb asked totally shocked.

"Yep, she sure did!" Ryder replies, "Turns out she's no stranger to keeping her kids in line. Just ask Kailee. To make matters worse, her and my mom are now good friends. They do yoga, play tennis together, and she comes over here a lot. I'm sure my mom will fill her in on everything that just happened with Dillon."

Ryder continues and nervously chuckles to try and hide his embarrassment, "Even to this day, she comments whenever she sees me.

"Hi Ryder, how's school? Behaving yourself?"
"She gives me that same smirk as the day my mom and her spanked me. I still get totally embarrassed whenever I see her." Ryder adds.

Caleb, in total shock, formulates a response, "Yeah, I can see why. It's one thing to have your ass exposed to your mom... But damn, your penis? To a neighbor? And then get spanked by her as well... I can't even imagine… That's so embarrassing."

Ryder laughs again, "Yep, but dude, my mom's a nurse, remember? She sees naked bodies all day, every day, in every color, gender, shape and size. She's totally desensitized. Plus, when it comes to her correcting our bad behavior, she's only interested in one thing… teaching us a lesson and reddening our butts."

Chapter 4

Shortly after dinner, Ryder said goodnight and he went inside to pack for his camping trip. Caleb also retreated to his house as well. There was only one problem… He couldn't stop thinking about Mrs. Doyle and this totally different side of her that he witnessed. He was super impressed with the way Ryder talked about his mom. There is a level of respect and love that Ryder has for her that is totally heartwarming. It actually makes Caleb a bit sad as he reflects on his own upbringing and the relationship he has with his parents, primarily his mom. Of course, he loves them, but he realizes that they never provided that type of structure or discipline. Especially not in the same manner that Mrs. Doyle disciplines her sons.

Something comes over him as he reflects on all the stupid things he's ever done. Everything from getting bad grades in school, hanging with the wrong crowd, mouthing off to bosses, quitting jobs, and even his relationships with girls might have been different and yielded even better results if he had more structure and discipline in his life. He thinks to himself that type of discipline surely would have helped him avoid some of the pitfalls he dealt with in the past.

He turns to his computer and starts entering keywords like "Spanking, Discipline, and Punishment." His computer screen is plastered with links to websites, videos, forums, and stories. He takes time to filter out the ones he doesn't want and finds himself visiting the websites and forums of people that are pro spanking. Caleb scans the many threads and articles written by people all over the world. There seems to be a good variety of interaction and threads. He reads through several discussions written by dads, moms, aunts, teachers, boyfriends, babysitters. He even reads several written by high-level bosses, employers, and government officials of various countries.

He quickly realizes that a few of these discussions are pure sexual garbage, but none the less, he scans through them, and chooses the ones to read in depth. Of course, just witnessing Mrs. Doyle in action, as a disciplinarian, makes him focuses primarily on the forum threads written by moms and women. These really get his attention as they discuss everything from the positions used when they administer a spanking, to the implements, the benefits, and the way it helps them run their households. They all seem to mention that it is very effective at immediately correcting unruly behavior.

Caleb is a total believer. Especially since he had just witnessed how Mrs. Doyle quickly gave Dillon an attitude adjustment, that immediately stopped his errant behavior. Within seconds, he finds his penis has returned to a full-on erection. Of course, he's also thinking, fantasizing, and visualizing Mrs. Doyle as he reads every one of these articles. Caleb quickly makes movies in his mind of her totally disciplining him, using every position and implement that he reads about on his bare backside. It doesn't stop there, as he also fantasizes about her in a romantic way as well. He pictures kissing her full, plush lips, touching every inch of her womanly curves, and having sex in every position possible!

He's beyond intrigued and continues to view other websites of Disciplinarians, Mistresses, fetish groups, spanking events, and even a few Dominatrix in his area. Once again, he feels his lower region totally throbbing. He now slips his sweat pants and underwear back down and starts vigorously masturbating.

Caleb has his computer screen displaying a picture that he found on one of the "Mom Spanking" sites. It's an illustration of a pretty mom using a thick leather strap and giving a spanking to her athletic, teenage son. The picture already shows the teenager with several red stripes across his bare bottom as the mom has the strap raised over her head ready to add more. The picture is so similar to what Caleb just witnessed a few hours ago with Mrs. Doyle spanking her son, that it blows his mind. As his eyes focus intently on the image, he visualizes himself in that picture on the receiving end. That's all it took, as his entire body shook like it was in an earthquake. Within seconds, he erupts into another climax, leaving his well defined abs covered in his juices.

Having just turned twenty-two years old, Caleb doesn't quite know what his next step is. Although he knows one thing for sure... he wants Mrs. Doyle, in more ways than one, in his life. He also knows the way he views his pretty next door neighbor has now changed forever.

Chapter 5

After being totally enthralled in a number of websites and videos, from spanking to full-on BDSM, Caleb, finally managed to get some sleep. He now wakes up to a beautiful sunshine-filled Saturday morning. As he lays in bed, his mind replays everything that he witnessed with Mrs. Doyle in his garage yesterday. He can't believe this is the same loving, friendly, neighbor next door that's always so pleasant and warm. To see this totally different side of her in action and to further hear his friend, her oldest son Ryder, elaborate on some of the spankings that his mom gave him, had really made an impact on Caleb.

He realizes that ever since yesterday he's totally infatuated with her. So much so, that he's actually fantasizing about her disciplining him, hard, in the same exact way as he witnessed. He pops out of bed complete with a morning erection as he hears the sounds of his neighbors in the driveway. He peaks through the blinds on his window in an incognito fashion. He sees Mr. Doyle and Ryder load the car with their camping supplies.

It's obvious they're moments away from leaving as they close the hatch of their SUV and get inside. As of yet, there's no sign of Ryder's younger brother Dillon. Caleb couldn't help wondering if Mrs. Doyle grounded him from going camping this weekend. He continues to nervously spy out the window, making sure that he stays hidden from view. Moments later, he sees Mrs. Doyle as she walked out with her arm around Dillon. She's dressed in her exercise clothes and has a bag draped over her shoulder with a pickle ball paddle and a tennis racquet peeking out.

Caleb focuses on how incredibly attractive Mrs. Doyle looks with her short, brown hair stylishly pinned-up, and just gracing her shoulders. He manages to take a good look and now, even more so, he really admires the sight of her curvy hips and full, round, ample bottom. That ass of hers is really outstanding as it totally fills-out and accentuates her thin, black leggings. For the first time, he also notices how toned and strong her arms look today. Maybe it's just the way he watched her easily handle her disobedient son and swing that strap yesterday. Maybe it's the way she held him firmly in place and dished out the discipline, but either way, today Caleb's fully taking notice.

He always thought Mrs. Doyle was pretty but he never really gave much attention to any woman that was twice his age. His only focus up until now had been bagging as many of the real cute college girls that he could... And there had been many. With a body that resembles a Greek God, and a stunning face, one thing was for sure... Caleb Wynn hasn't had a problem attracting girls. That's all changed since yesterday and right now his mind is focused on one woman. He's now totally engulfed with Mrs. Doyle as he continues to view her in a completely different way.

He does his best to put his ear to the window screen in order to hear what Mrs. Doyle is saying. He manages to hear her tell Dillon to behave himself this weekend during his camping trip with his dad and Ryder.

"If Ryder or your dad tells me that you misbehaved this weekend your next trip will be over my lap." She warns her son, "Is that clear?"

Caleb watches as Dillon nods his head with a "Yes" motion. He then sees Mrs. Doyle give her son a kiss on his cheek and a gentle pat on his butt over his jeans. The nurturing but firm reminder has Caleb's manhood pulsing thru his underwear. He watches as they pull out of the driveway and she waves goodbye. She proceeds to walk over to her own car and pulls out her cell phone.

"Hey Marcy, I'm leaving now. See you on the court."

Caleb hears her say before she gets into her car and pulls away. He figured she was heading to the park to play tennis or pickle ball since she was already carrying her bag. It's also clear that she's playing with Mrs. Beck, as Ryder told him yesterday, how they're now the best of friends. He takes a quick shower, but this time he doesn't relieve himself, and then quickly gets dressed in his gym shorts and t-shirt. He's totally infatuated with Mrs. Doyle and decides to head to the park to shoot some baskets. If his theory is right, she'll be there playing tennis, and he'll manage to steal some glimpses of her in action, swinging her racquet.

Caleb arrives at the park and his theory is dead on. Mrs. Doyle is on the court with Mrs. Beck and two other women. It's even better than Caleb imagined, as the women are playing pickle ball and handling their large paddles. He sees Mrs. Doyle firmly gripping her paddle, running, and swinging intensely, connecting with the ball. Mrs. Beck is also impressing him as he watches her swing the paddle with force as well.

His mind quickly fantasizes about getting stripped down to his birthday suit and spanked by both of these mature women. The details of Ryder's spanking from them really stuck in his mind as he pictures himself getting his ass thoroughly reddened that same way by both of them.

"How can this be?" He says to himself and wonders.

He never even thought about spanking or pictured his neighbor Mrs. Doyle in this way. For him, it's been the usual get as many blow jobs and fuck as many girls as possible. His attraction was always to girls his age or at least close to his age. He's never, ever, viewed older women in this manner. Furthermore, the thought of getting spanked by an older woman had never even crossed his mind until yesterday. Now his head is filled with images of Mrs. Doyle and even Mrs. Beck pulling his pants down and disciplining him.

Caleb dribbles the basketball, shoots another basket, and retrieves the ball as his eyes continue to gaze at his neighbors on the court. He's not only focused on the way they're swinging their paddles but also the way their asses shake as they run after the ball. Mrs. Doyle's curvy hips and slightly chubby ass has his penis more than throbbing again underneath his shorts. Mrs. Beck's toned arms and slightly thinner yoga physique also has him taking notice.

Mrs. Doyle retrieves the ball as she gets ready to serve. She inadvertently glances toward the basketball and notices Caleb, "Hi Caleb, good morning." She smiled and waved.

Mrs. Beck also smiles and waves at him. Caleb waves back at both of them and comments, "Good morning. You guys are crushing it!"

His slang expression makes the women chuckle, as they know from their own teenagers that this is a compliment. He goes back to dribbling the basketball, taking shots all over the court, and stealing glances of his neighbors. After an hour or so, their pickle ball game came to an end. Both women pack up their paddles and head to their cars, laughing and carrying-on. They pass by the basketball court and Mrs. Doyle takes a moment to stop and talk to Caleb.

"Hey Caleb, how are you today?"

"I'm good, thanks." he replies, "How are you guys?"
"Did you have a good game?"

"Yes, actually we did. We won again!" Mrs. Doyle excitedly answered.

Mrs. Beck chimes in, "One thing is for sure… we really know how to swing our paddles, right Megan?"

"We sure do, Marcy!" She laughs and smirks at Mrs. Beck.

Caleb's penis makes an involuntary pulse as a result of the women's paddle comment. He places the basketball over the front of his shorts to try and cover the bulge forming beneath them.

"Caleb, I wanted to apologize to you for disciplining my son in your garage." Mrs. Doyle expresses in a sincere tone. "You didn't need to have your workout with Ryder interrupted like that." She turns to her friend to explain her apology to Caleb.

"He really got an eyeful yesterday, Marcy. I gave Dillon a good strapping in his garage before I got him home."

"Oh, I see." Mrs. Beck nods as she gives her friend a smirk and adds, "Well, Megan... sometimes you got to do what you got to do."

"You're right, Marcy. I gave him a chance but Dillon decided he was way too cool to listen to his mom."

"Oh boy!" Mrs. Beck smirks, "We all know what that will lead to. Did your leather strap come out?"

"It sure did!" Mrs. Doyle nodded and continued to explain, "He was really acting up. He was being totally disrespectful, totally misbehaving, and just out of control. I really did a number on his fanny, and unfortunately, it happened right before Caleb's eyes, while he and Ryder were working out!"

"No need to apologize, Mrs. Doyle," Caleb assured her, "Ryder and I tried to tell him to come home but he was really trying act all tough in front of the girls. Then to have him run his mouth and call his brother those names… Ryder could've knocked his lights out!"

Caleb continued, "I'm sure he learned his lesson. You really put him in his place."

"Well, you should know that he got it even worse when I got him into the house. He was even so bold as to run and lock his bedroom door!" Mrs. Doyle carried on, "Talk about being a brat!"

"Ut Oh! Not smart to try that with a spanking mom!" Mrs. Beck quickly piped in, "Just ask my daughter what happened when she tried that with me!"

Caleb is literally getting his mind blown to smithereens as these two stunning but very stern moms continue to talk about spanking so openly.

Mrs. Doyle smirked at Marcy and replied, "Of course that didn't work. So this time, once I got hold of him, I completely stripped him down."

"MmmHmmm!" Mrs. Beck nodded in approval as she chimed in and briefly interrupted.

Mrs. Doyle gave her a confirming head nod, "Yep!... right down to his birthday suit. He got another dose of my strap. Then I marched him into the bathroom and washed his mouth out with soap. I also gave him a few with the wooden spoon, when I marched him back into his bedroom. He'll think twice before pulling a stunt like that again!"

"Well, we both know, nothing straightens out bad behavior like a good old-fashion bare bottom strapping." Mrs. Beck adds in a stern, convincing voice as her eyes quickly give Caleb's hot, athletic body a quick look over, "or a good dose of the wooden spoon!"

She then adds, "My house my rules. My motto is... you're never too old for a good spanking!"

Mrs. Doyle firmly nods, "That's the motto in my house also," she sarcastically laughs and adds, "Just ask Ryder... He got a serious strapping last month for drinking at school."

Caleb had already heard all about his last night directly from Ryder. Right now, he's doing all he can to keep the basketball on the front of his shorts in order to conceal his erection.

"Oh yes Megan, I remember that strap of yours. It made quite an impression on Ryder's bottom when he hit that baseball through my window. He got it good from both of us that day!" Mrs. Beck chuckles, "It's the reason why I purchased that same strap to use on my daughter."

"Here's the way I look at it..." Mrs. Doyle explains her reasoning, "I would rather be the one to give my kids a sore hiney than have them get their teeth knocked out by some big jock at school. Especially Dillon, his mouth has already got him into a few fights and I'm just not having it!"

Caleb can't help it and he smirks again since he knows all the details of both of those spankings. He also couldn't help but respond to Mrs. Doyle's last comment.

"That makes perfect sense, Mrs. Doyle," Caleb added,"I definitely got into my share of fights that I should have avoided. Your kids are lucky to have you as their mom."

Mrs. Doyle turns to Caleb with a huge smile and a sincerity in her voice, "Thank you for understanding, honey. By the way, I baked you a little something so stop by later this afternoon. It's my way of apologizing."

"Sure, thank you Mrs. Doyle. See ya' later." Caleb confirmed with a smile.

Of course, by now, after hearing all this talk from both of these super hot moms, Caleb's penis was really throbbing. Luckily, he had that basketball in place to hide the tent that popped up in the front of his shorts. His knees even wobbled a bit as he focused on the two stunning women's rear-ends. Their round, plump butts jiggled perfectly from side to side as they walked towards their cars.

Caleb realizes that this afternoon, with Megan Doyle's entire family away for the weekend, he'll be alone with her. His mind quickly wandered to the unlikely scenario of passionately kissing her. He also formed vivid images in his mind of just bending her over the kitchen table, grabbing onto those curvy hips of hers, and fucking the daylights of her.

Mrs. Doyle and Mrs. Beck arrived at their cars and stopped for a moment. Marcy was just waiting for Megan to make one of her humorous comments about Caleb, especially with a body like that. After all, the two of them are regulars at a shop downtown, near the college, where they're used to gawking at the athletic hunks.

Mrs. Beck didn't wait any longer, and was the first to joke, "Okay… So which one was the basketball? That thing he was holding or that

round bubble under the back of his shorts! My God! What a cutie...
And that ass!"

Megan non-nonchalantly responded, "Yeah, he is cute, and a nice
boy. He and Ryder have been great friends since high school."

"Meg!" Mrs. Beck excitedly responded, "That's all you have to say?
First of all, he's not a boy, and he's every bit as hot as the college
athletes we drool over... Did you see those muscles? Did you see
that ass?"

Megan laughs at Marcy's humor, "Oh yeah, I noticed it. He was
doing squats yesterday when I went into the garage after Dillon. It
damn near poked my eye out!"

"That's my girl!" Marcy replied with laughter, "It's not like you to
hold back and not comment on a cute ass like that!"

"Well, asses always get me in trouble." Mrs. Doyle jokes,
"Although, it's usually my fat ass that really gets me in trouble."

"Haha!" Marcy laughs, "Well Meg, you do have one hell of an ass!"

Marcy gives Megan's body a thorough look over, "Look at that
thing! You make me want to slap your ass!"

"Haha! Don't tempt me Marcy, you know how much I miss that!"
Megan laughs, "I told you all about my college days... God!... Those
times were amazing!"

"You sure did!" Marcy confirmed, "You and that professor... The
way he disciplined you... Hot as can be!"

Megan nods, "It was!... What I wouldn't do to have an ounce of that
again... That fire... that kink... that pure adrenaline rush... that
feeling of being desired. I miss that, Marcy."

"Yeah, I know, sis, "Mrs. Beck nods, "My husband is usually asleep
on the couch by 8pm!"

Mrs. Doyle responds, "Well Jim, never had that in him anyway. Sex was never one of his strong points... but hey, it made us two amazing boys. He's an amazing dad and has always been a great provider, but let's face it, after 22 years of marriage, I don't look at him in that sexual way."

"I hear you," Mrs. Beck replied, "Let's go grab a coffee. I'm in the mood to look at hot guys!"

"Me too!" Mrs. Doyle responded, "Hot guys with even hotter asses!"

"There ya' go! Now that's the Megan Doyle I know!" Mrs. Beck added as they got into their cars and headed to the coffee shop.

Chapter 6

After another hour or so, Caleb returns home from shooting baskets in the park and heads into his garage for a workout. Thankfully, his erection subsided and he goes thru a killer workout for at least another hour and a half. After grabbing lunch, he hits the shower, changes into clean clothes, and walks through his yard over to Mrs. Doyle's house.

He rings the bell and within a few seconds she opens the door and greets him with her huge, pearly white smile. Not only does she look impeccable as her body easily fills out another pretty sundress, she smells absolutely amazing. Caleb's eyes almost pop out of his head and his knees buckle as she swings the door fully open and lets him in. She offers to make coffee and after he agrees, they both take a seat at the kitchen table. Mrs. Doyle presents a tray of fresh pastries along with a container filled with chocolate baked goodies.

"Caleb, these are protein bars that I baked for you. It's my way of apologizing once again for fully exposing Dillon and spanking him in front of you yesterday. I should've refrained and marched him into my house and dealt with him behind closed doors." Mrs. Doyle continues, "I was beyond frustrated with him and my temper just came out. Both of my sons know the consequences and that I don't tolerate disrespect and errant behavior from them. It doesn't happen often, but sometimes there's no other way than to give them a good bare bottom strapping." She tells him.

Caleb responds, "It's no sweat Mrs. Doyle, you're an amazing mom. In fact, Ryder and I had an in-depth conversation over dinner last night. The way he talked about you was so enlightening that it brought tears to my eyes. You should be really proud of him and Dillon as well. You raised amazing kids that love and respect you."

Caleb paused for moment then continued, "So, even if they misbehave once in a while, they know there will be consequences for their actions. Ryder especially told me how he needs that structure and accountability to keep him focused, especially now at college.

Otherwise, he might make even more stupid mistakes and get into real trouble."

Mrs. Doyle's face turns a slight shade of pink as her cheek fully blushed. The way Caleb just relayed that message really struck a nerve in her as a few tears formed in her pretty, blue eyes.

Caleb continues, "Ryder told me all the details of the spanking that he received last month when he got caught drinking on campus. He also told me about a few more spankings that you've given him over the years, including the baseball incident and the double disciplining that he received several years ago from you and Mrs. Beck."

"He told you all that?" She asks.

"He sure did… willingly. It actually made me sad not to have that type of structure, discipline, and accountability from my parents. I mean, I know they love me, but they were never strict like that. They just grounded me or took away the car, my phone, etc. I could've avoided so many pitfalls if they were more strict with me. Maybe I wouldn't have dropped out of college after getting my Associates Degree. Maybe I wouldn't have quit several of my past jobs or gotten fired for mouthing off to my bosses. Hell, I won't even get into my love life and my relationships with girls. Let's just say none of them last more than a few months." admitted Caleb, with a sincere tone.

"Hmmm, I see." Mrs. Doyle replies, "So you were never spanked in your whole life?"

"Nope… Never." Caleb responds, "It was never even on my radar. Now I have to admit that after seeing the way you corrected Dillon's behavior with that strap, and after hearing Ryder tell me all the details of his past spankings from you, it just makes me wonder." He continues with a perplexed look on his face.

"I mean, did my parents just not care enough?" He asks, but then continues, "I know to this day they would still provide me with whatever I need. However, maybe this lack of discipline is the reason that I often disrespected my elders, my teachers, and lost jobs by mouthing off to bosses. I have absolutely no filter at times and my mouth really gets me in trouble. So much of this might have been avoided if I had more accountability… more discipline."

Chapter 7

Mrs. Doyle listens intently. She can't help but be impressed with his maturity and the way that Caleb is expressing himself. Especially on subjects like spanking and discipline. It's obvious that he's given a good amount of thought to his past behavior and how discipline and accountability could have helped him throughout the years. She also can't help being a little revved up sitting there in her kitchen with this hot guy in front of her. She's undressed him at least 5 times so far with her eyes. After all, she had just returned from recapping her glory days, looking at college heartthrobs, and talking about all kinds of kinky fantasies with her best friend Marcy over coffee.

Her mind can't help but create some fantasies of clearing off her kitchen table and having crazy sex right here, right now, with him. In addition, with all this talk about spanking, she also created several fantasies in her mind of getting at his cute, muscle-toned, round ass with her leather strap. She finally snaps out of it, and regains her composure. Her big blue eyes maintained contact with him and she went on, in her usual nurturing and loving manner, to offer some motherly type of advice.

"Caleb, I'm sure your parents care and love you immensely. Some parents spank their kids and others just don't. I happen to be a mom that won't hesitate to do that." She relays, "I found nothing works as good as a leather strap across a bare bottom. It does wonders for correcting bad behavior." She ends with a slight giggle and her cute trademark smirk, "Lord knows, that's the way my mom took it to my plump butt!"

Caleb takes notice and replies, "Mrs. Doyle, I have even more respect and admiration for you. I mean you're not only an amazing mom, a warm neighbor, but you're also a strong, no-nonsense woman as well."

He continued, "And I think you're right. Dillon, will get his teeth knocked out if he doesn't look out. He's going to mouth off to the wrong guy in high school or down the line in college. He'll really pay the price. So you, putting him in his place at this age, is the right thing to do."

"You are way beyond your years, Caleb. I'm super impressed that you came to this realization." She commented with a smile.

Caleb's tone and philosophical introspection really impresses Mrs. Doyle. She takes a sip of her coffee and lets her mind formulate a response. She delivers a heartfelt message using the most nurturing, motherly tone that she can muster. She touches his hand and looks straight into his eyes.

"I want you to focus on all the good you've accomplished, even with those past setbacks. You can't change the past, but you can take steps to ensure your future is on the right path and the way you want it."

She continues, "Ryder told me about your new job... Congratulations, that's amazing! When do you actually start, honey?"

"I'm still in my old position but I start my new position as soon as I pass my drug test and physical exam. That's not going to be a problem, since I don't do drugs, smoke pot, and I rarely have a drink. Most of the time I'm eating healthy and chugging protein drinks." He chuckles as he looks at her.

"Well, once you get the paperwork, I can help. I can write you a script for your drug test and blood work. We can go over the results and I can even do your physical exam and everything else. I can even administer the new vaccines and flu shots. Most employers strongly suggest them and some even make it mandatory." Mrs. Doyle tells him.

She couldn't help but notice a slight glow in Caleb's eyes as they suddenly opened wide. Caleb, on the other hand, can't conceal that he's thinking about it and giving her offer to examine him his full attention. His mind was already creating that movie of her hands probing and touching every inch of his body.

Mrs. Doyle continues in her nurturing way, "I know this might be awkward for you. It would require having me, your next door neighbor, and good friend's mom, seeing you completely naked. However, I assure you that it will stay between me and you. I can even do the physical in the privacy of your house or you can come here during my work hours. My boys are at school and Mr. Doyle is at work, so only you and I will know. It's up to you, with no pressure at all. If it's too close for comfort, I can still write your scripts and you can go to the doctor of your choice for your exam."

Caleb's legs squirm under the table as he feels his penis throb and harden again at the very thought of her examining him.

"Anyway, give it some thought, honey." She tells him, "I know it's a lot for a 21-year-old to take in over coffee, but I really am impressed with your maturity and introspection."

"I'm actually 22." Caleb chuckles and quickly replies, "My birthday was a few days ago."

"Really, a few days ago?" She smirks, "Well then... maybe I should give you your birthday spankings. Especially, since you've never been spanked before." She sarcastically giggled and blurted out of nowhere.

She actually can't believe that she said that. She realizes that she's now actually flirting with her next-door neighbor. A guy that's half her age, and is one of her son's best friends.

Caleb's penis goes into a full erection beneath his pants after hearing her offer. He's momentarily lost for words, which is something that he doesn't experience often, since he usually has an answer for everything.

He takes a deep breath and asks, "Mrs. Doyle, can I tell you something in confidence?"

She maintains a loving grip on his hand and responds, "Of course, honey. You have my word. Whatever you tell me will stay between me and you. No one will know, not even my son, Ryder, or my best friend Marcy… I promise."

Caleb takes another deep, cleansing breath to calm his nervousness, and then begins to speak, "okay… here goes..."

He continues with a slight tremble in his voice, "Mrs. Doyle, something awakened in me after I watched you spank Dillon yesterday. I think that bare bottom spankings as a method of punishment like you use on your own boys, might actually work wonders for me. It's something that I never had before and I think it would be instrumental for me. Especially as I begin my professional career, and maybe even head back to college for night classes. It might really help to keep me focused and in line."

"Hmm, I see." Mrs. Doyle responds, as she's still holding his hands.

Caleb doesn't wait and continues to explain, "You see Mrs. Doyle, when I talked to Ryder yesterday, he gave me all the details on how you use spankings to keep him in line. This really intensified my need to find out more about spanking and discipline and how it might help me. I went straight to my computer last night and started searching "Spanking", "Discipline", "Moms that spank", etc. I visited several websites on those subjects."

"Really?" Mrs. Doyle now blinks hard hearing this.

Caleb continues, "Of course, I came across the hardcore BDSM, Dungeons, Dominatrix sites and videos. However, I also came across purely spanking forums run by moms, spanking and fetish events, and even the websites of several Disciplinarians in our area. I actually emailed a few of them and I've gotten some responses back!"

Caleb pauses and takes a deep breath, "Phew! I'm slightly nervous telling you all this."

He takes a moment and tries to get his nervousness and all his senses under control.

Mrs. Doyle chimes in and expresses, "Wow! You did all that? You really went all in, Caleb."

Caleb responds, "I guess what I'm trying to say is that I need to experience a real, disciplinary spanking from a woman that knows how to administer it. It's something that can't be sexual or given to me by girls my age…. or even a Dominatrix. That's a whole different vibe and scenario. This spanking has to be authentic. It has to be administered from an older, more mature woman, preferably a mom that spanks… Like you!"

He totally confesses and lets out a deep breath to relieve the nervous pressure that was forming in his chest. Caleb feels a sense of relief and he decides to continue and comes right out and asks for it.

"Mrs. Doyle, I know you may have been joking, but instead of getting a birthday spanking..." he pauses for a second, "I would like to experience the same type of spanking that you gave Dillon yesterday."

Mrs. Doyle's big, blue eyes opened wide. She doesn't say a thing just yet, but instead, responds by tilting her head down and raising her eyebrows.

Chapter 8

"Really?" She asks him in a tone that is beyond surprised.

"Yes, Ma'am… Full force with your strap, but not in front of anyone... Just me and you. I think it would be a valuable lesson for me and it would totally help me experience that type of discipline." He looks at her even more intently, yet still with a level of innocence and asks.

"Is that something you would consider?" He concludes with a sigh, feeling slightly out of breath.

Mrs. Doyle is a smart woman. As an APRN, she's one level below a Doctor, and as a mom to 2 boys, there's not much that gets by her. She knows all about the hormones that young men Caleb's age experience and this spanking desire may be sexual as well. She even feels he may have developed a slight crush on her. The feeling is kind of mutual, as she's also experiencing some tingles throughout regions of her body. She takes a moment to formulate her response and expresses it with full honesty.

"Caleb, just so you know, I have never spanked anyone but my own kids." She responds. "I need to tell you a story about me when I was your age." She continues.

"I was raised from a strict family and I was spanked bare bottom by both my mom and dad. That's where I got spanking as a method of discipline from. When I went away to college I found myself getting into all kinds of trouble because I had no one to answer to. I was around your age and during one of my semesters I developed a huge crush on my professor, Mr. Roberts. He was older, about forty-five, somewhere around the age I am now. He was fit, strong, and very handsome. I didn't care that he was married, had kids, or anything else. All I thought about each day was him. I even masturbated daily to the thoughts of him spanking me." Mrs. Doyle now takes a deep, cleansing, breath before continuing.

"I purposely flunked a test and caused enough mischief in class that it earned me a detention. Back in those days, you would be held after school for several hours, studying, and making up for bad grades, with the teacher present. Mr. Roberts knew this was out of character for me. Without me even knowing, he called my mom and learned of my strict upbringing. During the detention, he flat out asked me why I was acting up. This was my chance to fulfill my fantasy, but even more so, to have the accountability that I desperately needed from being far away from home. I completely confessed and told him that I needed him to spank me to get me back on track. He wasn't dumb and he knew that I had a huge crush on him and some of this bordered on a sexual, coming-of-age type of experience that I was craving."

"WOW! Kinda like me..." Caleb responds as he realizes the similarities to what he's feeling for his neighbor.

"What happened? Did he actually spank you?" He asks her.

"Oh, he sure did!" She chuckles and further explains, "Back in my days there were no cell phones or cameras and people in authority had no problem dishing out discipline. Especially at a private college like the one I attended. He took me by the arm and escorted me into the large back room attached to the classroom. It was essentially a huge closet that had some supplies and a couple of chairs. On the wall there were several paddles hanging down, plus a strap like the one I use now, and even several canes. For this first spanking, he put me over his lap, lifted my skirt, and pulled my panties down. That hand spanking he gave me was every bit as hard as any hand spanking that I've received from my mom and dad. Even though I wanted it and I fantasized about it, it was still punishment and it hurt like hell. My rear-end was red and bruised for days."

Caleb is totally floored hearing Mrs. Doyle tell the events of her college year. He excitedly fires question after question at her without waiting for her to respond.

"So was it everything you hoped for?"
"I mean, did it give you relief?"

"Did you still masturbate and think about him?"
"Did you ever cross the line with him romantically or sexually?" Caleb rapidly inquires.

Mrs. Doyle giggles at his quick onslaught of questions, then she responds.

"No, we never crossed the line romantically or sexually, but I would have." She continues, "Mr. Roberts always remained extremely professional and kept it purely about discipline. Having him discipline me absolutely helped me to maintain good grades and keep me focused. In addition, it gave me the sexual release I needed because it filled a fantasy of mine. At times I would still masturbate and think about him, but not as much. I was finally able to get more done because it was no longer consuming my every thought. I made my fantasy of him giving me a bare bottom spanking come to fruition, and I'm so glad I did. I really needed to experience that."

Caleb again realizes the similarity and how this is almost exact to the way he's feeling about Mrs. Doyle. He continues to listen intently to hear every word she says.

"What it also gave me, besides the sexual release, was the accountability and structure that I desperately needed. He had no problem spanking me if he felt I needed it. I also had an open door to go to him and ask for a spanking if I felt I was getting off track." Mrs. Doyle explains.

"So how many times did he spank you during that semester?" Caleb asks.

"At least a half dozen more throughout the semester. I received the strap once and even the cane when I got into a fight on campus. It straightened out my behavior and I never got into another fight during my remaining years." She answers.

"Wow!" Caleb replies, totally stunned.

"So, as you can see from my own experience, some of this may also be sexual for you. At least it was for me. However, it was extremely beneficial for giving me the discipline that I needed and for keeping my behavior in line." She expressed to him.

Mrs. Doyle nailed it and Caleb knew it. She summed it up perfectly and almost as if she was in his body. His mind constantly plays with the fantasy after fantasy of her and him together. Everything from having her aggressively pulling his pants down, and applying that leather strap to his bare ass, to having all kinds of kinky sex… from full-on raunchy, to oral, and even anal with her. His dick has been consistently hard, even after he's pleasured himself a number of times fantasizing about her.

"So Caleb," She looked directly into his big green eyes, "To answer your question… Yes, I will discipline you."

Chapter 9

Her response gets Caleb about as hard as he's ever been in his life. Right now, his penis is literally poking through the top of his sweat pants. It's a good thing he's sitting at the kitchen table with his lower body hidden from her.

Mrs. Doyle further elaborates, "Since this is something that you've asked for, I want you to tell me exactly the way you want me to handle you. You've done a great job at expressing yourself so far. So think about it and make sure this spanking accomplishes exactly what you want it to accomplish."

Caleb's mind is running a mile a minute yet he's totally clear on what he wants from Mrs. Doyle and quickly reiterates.

"Ryder told me all about the way you handle him when he gets in trouble. I want that thorough type of discipline from you. Just like what I witnessed yesterday, and even more. The way you changed Dillon's behavior in a matter of seconds blew my mind. He was rude, disrespectful, and just plain annoying. The minute you came into my garage clenching that leather strap, his attitude totally changed. The way you chased him into the corner, grabbed him, and gave him several hard swats with the strap straightened him out instantly!" Caleb tells her and continues.

"However, the kicker was when you yanked his pants and underwear down. I would never have believed it if I hadn't seen it for myself. I mean... Maybe it was the embarrassment and vulnerability of being fully exposed... Or maybe it was the way you painted red stripes on his rear-end with no mercy. You were fierce and relentless!"

Caleb now completely confesses, "It really turned me on... You turned me on! I can't stop thinking about that spanking... or you!"

Mrs. Doyle listens and even though she doesn't say a word, she's actually smiling inside. She's hiding it very well, but she's actually getting a little flustered also. Her mind had already undressed him a number of times as they were sitting there, chatting over coffee. She now feels a surge of her own wetness accumulate in her panties.

She knows this interaction is dangerous and it's far from being the right thing to do. He's her neighbor… One of her son's best friends! Even with all that, she also remembers what it was like for herself to have that craving when she was his age. Not to mention, it gave her a lifetime of hot, sexy, memories that still turns her on to this day! Make no mistake about it, Megan Doyle has a very kinky side to her that's been dormant for well over 20 years. Ever since her marriage, giving birth to her first child, even going back to night school to become an APRN. It seemed everything else took priority in her life and came before her sexual desires and fantasies. That untamed, free-spirited girl who loved and craved all kinds of wild sex, turned into a super mom, a tender nurturer, a caregiver, and at times a strict disciplinarian.

She thinks to herself that it was just a little over an hour ago, when she was telling Marcy how she wanted to be desired. She misses it so much and craves to have an ounce of that fire...that kink that she used to have in her life. Now here she is, with her young next-door neighbor, half her age, who is as hot-looking as you can get. And he's here, right in front of her, actually desiring her to strip him down and spank him. It's not that she enjoys spanking her kids, she does that only to correct their bad behavior. However, the thought of doing that and more to this sexy young man sitting before her is so appealing that it's totally blowing her mind. To this day, she absolutely loves to be handled forcefully, but it's something that her husband just doesn't have within him to do. On the same note, she equally loves being dominant and the one in control, and lord knows, she can really dish it out!

Mrs. Doyle hides her excitement behind a squinty-eyed smirk as she gains all the clarity she needs. Her mind is now completely focused on totally dominating Jordan and handling him with so much aggression, that it really has her heartbeat and her adrenaline pumping. She actually pinches herself to make sure that she's not dreaming and all this is really happening.

Caleb interrupted her thought process by chiming back in, "Mrs. Doyle, I feel the exact same way that you felt for your professor. Aside from wanting the structure and accountability, some of this is definitely sexual and a turn-on."

"I understand that perfectly... I lived it, honey, "Megan Doyle nods and replies, "For some people like myself, pain and pleasure go together really well."

"I realize that, Ma'am," Caleb admitted, "especially after I visited all those websites and watched a ton of spanking and even BDSM videos last night. I even created a profile on a couple of fetish sites."

"You're one sexy boy, Caleb Wynn," Mrs. Doyle added, "I meant man... One sexy man. 22 isn't a boy, you're a man and you know what you want. I applaud that... You've expressed yourself very well and I'm super impressed."

Caleb smirks, "Thank you. I may not understand it all right now, but I know one thing... and I want you to know one thing also... It's you! I want to experience this from you and no one else!"

Mrs. Doyle now can't help but display a cute, half-smile on her face. She feels so good to be wanted and have someone look at her in that way. It doesn't matter if it's sexually, or as a disciplinarian, Caleb made it clear that he craves her. This was all she needed to hear. Especially from a young guy with the face of a model and the physique of a Greek God. She's more than ready to give him what he wants. In fact, right now, she's thinking about reaching over the kitchen table, pulling him up by his earlobe, and yanking his pants down. After giving his ass a good strapping, she's fantasizing about kissing and licking every inch of his body, then fucking the daylights out of him!

She refrains and gets a grip on her emotions, "Okay sweetheart... I understand completely. You want me to give you the same exact spanking that I gave Dillon... You're sure about this?"

"Yes Ma'am... totally!"

She asks Caleb as she raises her eyebrows, in a stern but very sexy way, "You know I'll be pulling down your pants in your garage?"

Caleb nodded yes without saying a word.

"Well, it didn't end with just a couple swats of my strap to his bare bottom in your garage," Mrs. Doyle relayed.

She went on, "When I got him back here in the house, I stripped him down to his birthday suit and gave him several more with my strap. Then I took him into the bathroom and thoroughly washed his mouth out with soap. I finished up by giving him a few with the wooden spoon on his bed, before I grounded him for the evening."

Mrs. Doyle continued to look straight into Caleb's eyes after she relayed all that information. She noticed that he didn't even blink. It was clear that he was totally convinced and totally focused on getting disciplined by her. Now, the anticipation of getting at his amazing body is actually turning her on… big time! That feeling of being in control, and the feeling of power, makes her take on a totally different dynamic with him. She's no longer the tender, warm neighbor, calmly talking about all this with him over coffee. The tone of voice quickly changes, and she becomes very stern and very serious.

She now scolded him with that fierce tone of hers, "Once I get you back in this house, I'll be stripping every piece of clothing off you! You'll be completely naked, without a stitch of fabric on that body of yours, young man! I'm going to have you dancing leg to leg from my strap!"

She really raises her voice, "Am I making myself clear?"

Caleb hears the sternness in her voice and replies with a slight tremble, "Yes, Ma'am!"

"I'm also going to wash your mouth out with soap and apply another shade of red to those cheeks with my wooden spoon!" She tells him in that stern tone, "That cute fanny of yours is in for it, mister!"

The sudden change in her tone sent shivers up his spine. He watches as she gets up from the kitchen table and walks in the direction of her bedroom. Her ass looks insatiable as it jiggles underneath her pretty, thin sundress with every step she takes. She comes back to the kitchen clenching the thick leather strap in her hand. This vision of his pretty neighbor holding the strap with a stern look on her face, instantly gave him goose bumps.

"Stand up, young man!" She ordered him.

Caleb instantly obeys and stands facing her. He's a few inches taller than his pretty neighbor and tilts his head slightly downward to maintain eye contact with her.

"Caleb, I want you to take your sneakers and socks off." She instructs him.

Caleb follows through and notices that he's now only a little taller than her, especially since she has two inch heels on. Mrs. Doyle takes her finger and places it under Caleb's chin.

"I'm going to give you the exact spanking that you asked for. If at any time, for any reason, you change your mind and want me to stop, simply say the word 'RED'... Understand?"

"Yes, Mrs. Doyle. I understand." He replies.

She then instructed him, "Go to your garage and wait for me. I will be there in a few minutes." She instructs.

Chapter 10

Caleb leaves his socks and sneakers in place, walks out of her house barefoot, and retreats to his garage. He can't believe this is about to happen. In a few moments he's going to be at the receiving end of her thick, leather strap. His stomach feels as if one thousand butterflies are in it flapping around. His penis is still fully erect and hidden beneath his exercise pants. He's just moments away from having her pull them down and fully exposing him. The thought of being stripped bare by his beautiful, next-door neighbor is already a turn on, let alone the thought of her reddening his ass. The anticipation is overwhelming as he glances out the open garage door in the rear of his house.

He watches as Mrs. Doyle walks through his isolated backyard firmly gripping the strap in her right hand. His nerves take over and he's actually frozen in the center of his garage. It's just about the exact spot that her son Dillon was in until he foolishly tried to back away and resist when she approached. Mrs. Doyle enters the garage, gives Caleb a stern look, and taps the strap on the palm of her hand.

That stern but incredibly sexy, get-down-to-business-look, coupled with those curves of her hips as she faces him head on, is enough to make him explode. At this very moment, his erection had reached an all-time high in his life as Mrs. Doyle scowls her eyes at him.

"It's time to address this behavior of yours, Caleb." She scolds and slowly approaches him. This causes him to instantly take one step back.

"Oh, you can try to back up and resist all you want, young man… but one way or another I'm going to get at that rear-end of yours... I'm going to give you a spanking you'll always remember!"

That scolding was about as sexy as it can get coming from the stern mom. It set the tone and added to the punishment that Caleb was about to get. His heart is now beating a mile a minute as he looks at her with that more than stern expression on her pretty face. The wait is finally over and Mrs. Doyle springs into action and moves in quickly, just like she did with her son Dillon. She reaches out and grabs Caleb's left arm, and spins him around. Then, without any hesitation whatsoever, she forcefully swings the thick leather strap.

The strap makes a muted thud sound as it lands over Caleb's exercise pants. Even though the heavy cotton fabric took away some of pain from the impact, Caleb still felt a good sting. He naturally tucked his body inward and away from her as the strap landed across his right butt cheek. Mrs. Doyle forcefully spins him around again and raises the strap high in the air. She swings the strap hard and this time it connects square in the middle of his rear end.

Caleb felt this one more as was in a bit shocked that it hurt so much through his clothes. He manages to pull his arm free from her and quickly covers his bottom. He takes several steps away from her as a natural reaction. Mrs. Doyle has seen this all before and once again she simply wasn't having it. She's been through this with her boys and one thing is for sure, she knows how to handle resistance.

"Move that hand, Mister!" She scolds, and without any delay, she delivers another hard swat that really connects over his sweat pants.

Caleb definitely felt the force of the strap over his pants. Unable to hold it in, he let his pain be known by making a small sound.

"Ow!" Lightly escapes from his mouth as his hands once again reach back to clench his butt.

Mrs. Doyle sees her opportunity and wastes no time. This is the moment she's been waiting for as she quickly moves in and backs him into the corner of the garage. Standing face to face with him, she abruptly reaches down, slides her finger into the waistband of his clothing, and gives a swift, forceful pull. This causes his exercise pants to fall along with his underwear below his knees. Caleb's penis is rock hard and totally pointing north. He does his best and now shifts his hands to cover and hide the embarrassment of having the sexy mom next-door see him with a super enormous hard on.

Mrs. Doyle tries her best to act completely un-phased and maintain her focus on disciplining him. She reaches down, grabs his wrists, and assertively pulls his hands away. As she succeeds at moving his hands away from covering himself, her eyes totally light up as she takes in the sight of his beautiful dick.

Caleb can't help from feeling embarrassed as he watches his neighbor's attention shift to his penis. Once her eyes get their fill of gazing at it, she grabs his arm, spins him back around with his cute, round, tush facing out to her. She then uses some additional force to push and hold him into the corner.

With Caleb facing the wall and unable to see her, Mrs. Doyle lets out a smile that spans from ear to ear. She was always an ass-lover and she absolutely loves the sight of Caleb's toned bare bottom. She eyes Caleb's sexy, athletic bottom like it's a target. Her smile then quickly changes as the vertical, frown lines between her eyebrows become more pronounced. She also purses her lips together as she's totally determined to give him the discipline that he asked for. Her eyes remain fixated on his bare bottom and the exact spot that she wants to redden with her strap. As she holds onto his left arm, she bends her torso and raises her leather strap high above her head. Mrs. Doyle then unleashes several relentless swings one after another, immediately adding more red stripes to Caleb's cheeks.

Caleb, for the first time in his life, feels the force of a leather strap across his bare bottom. He clenches his teeth to absorb the pain as his body involuntarily tucks inward.

"Stick out that fanny, Caleb!" Mrs. Doyle loudly scolds.

Those old-fashioned words that she uses to describe his ass make it even more turn-on, if that's possible. He now feels one hand of hers pressing into his abdomen while the other pulls on his hips to make his ass arch out. Mrs. Doyle now has him exactly where she wants him, and once again, she capitalizes on the opportunity. She takes one step back as she keeps her eyes focused like a laser on his bare bottom. Without any further hesitation, she forcefully administers several relentless swats with her strap. The sound of the leather connecting with Caleb's bare bottom, sounds like fireworks, as it echoes loudly off the concrete walls of the garage.

This time Caleb can't help it and lets out a slight moan as his feet, one by one, lift off the ground. He dances from leg to leg as his hands reach down to grip his bottom. He remembers seeing her son Dillon do this exact dance yesterday when he felt the wrath of her strap.

"Ouch! Oow!" Emanates from his mouth.

"Move those hands, mister!" Mrs. Doyle instructs her young neighbor. She takes another step back and gets a complete eyeful as Caleb's fully erect penis is a sight that just can't be ignored. Once again, she grabs his arm and spins him back around so that his rear-end is facing her in clear view. She couldn't help but let her fingers inspect and trace the bright, red marks that formed all over his cheeks. Caleb turns his head over his shoulder and takes in the view of his pretty neighbor running her fingers all over his ass cheeks to double check her work. His feeling of vulnerability and embarrassment is equally coupled with excitement as he remains totally rock hard and turned on by the way she's handling him.

"Pull up your pants and march into my house, young man!" Mrs. Doyle instructs him.

Chapter 11

Caleb quickly obliges without even saying a word. He exits his garage and walks over to her house and lets himself in. He's right back in her kitchen where this conversation first began.

He knows the second part of the spanking along with a mouth soaping is about to happen here. So far, it's exactly the way he witnessed Dillon getting it. The way she handled him, pulled his pants down, and administered that leather strap is actually better than his fantasy. The insane hard on that he's sporting is total proof of that. He wonders what Mrs. Doyle is thinking as she took in the full view of his penis along with his ass. He enters her kitchen and waits for her with butterflies still vigorously flapping around in his stomach.

Mrs. Doyle takes a few moments to compose herself as she remains in Caleb's garage. She definitely is feeling a bit over-heated from handling her hunky, young neighbor and seeing him in full bloom. She was totally honest in telling him that the only people she ever spanked in her entire life were her two sons. She knew she had a kinky side to herself, but there was no way she could have anticipated everything that she was feeling right now. That sexy, crazy, kinky side of her has just awakened after administering the strap to Caleb's bare bottom. She felt a pure rush of adrenaline from the moment she grabbed him, yanked his pants down, and marked his cute cheeks with bright, red stripes.

It's safe to say that giving her cute neighbor a serious strapping has made her wet beyond belief. She reaches down and touches her panties, which are completely moist from her own juices. Some kind of switch must have flipped in her mind because now she's viewing Caleb in a completely different way. She's actually really turned on and can't wait to go back into her home and to continue disciplining him.

Caleb's natural good looks and his killer physique easily draw the attention of every young girl and now he has a new admirer in her as well. Unable to contain herself, she gives in and rubs her vagina vigorously underneath her panties. She closes her eyes and replays numerous images of his sexy body getting disciplined by her. The image of his totally erect penis fills her head as she gasps and rubs herself harder. She stifles her moans as she recalls how absolutely beautiful Caleb's dick is. Her mind then fills with images of his cute, tight ass. Mrs. Doyle's always been an ass woman and now it's safe to say that Caleb's round, muscular bubble butt is total perfection and was made for spanking.

Mrs. Doyle knows that she's close to having an orgasm and uses all the restraint she can to pull her fingers away from her vagina. She straightens her sundress, grabs her strap, and heads out of Caleb's garage. The kitchen door swings opens as Caleb watches Mrs. Doyle entered with the leather strap once again firmly clenched in her hand.

"You wanted the exact spanking that I gave Dillon... right, Caleb?" She asks.

Caleb looks at her and nods his head with a YES motion.

"Very well!" She responds as she places one hand on his left bicep and the other on his earlobe. "This is where I took him after I got him out of his locked bedroom." She commands with a firm grip on him, "March!... right into the family room."

Once they get into the family room, she backs him into one of the corners of the room. She immediately tugs his pants and underwear back down, and this time she removes them completely off his body. Caleb then witnesses her fingers slide underneath his t-shirt as she pulls it completely off his torso and throws it onto the carpet. He's now standing there facing her, fully naked, without one stitch of clothing on his body. Caleb's mind is a mixed ball of mush as he experiences this feeling of complete embarrassment and total vulnerability. Mrs. Doyle reaches out and takes a firm grip on his left arm. She leads him toward the arm of the sofa and commands him.

"Bend... Rear end out and stay in position!" Her voice has a serious tone of authority that sends shivers up his spine.

He feels her fingers touch, then gently pull and guide his hips outward. This automatically makes his ass arch up even higher. Now, Mrs. Doyle has him exactly where she wants him. She takes a step back and then positions herself slightly off to his left side. She then extends her left arm onto the small of his back and presses down to hold him in place. Without further ado, she raises the strap, and delivers a forceful, fluid swing.

It connects to the lower portion of Caleb's bottom and slightly onto his upper legs. The sound bounces off the walls in her house as Caleb grits his teeth and stays in position.

"This will happen every time you misbehave or don't give 100% at work or school."
"Is that clear, mister?" She scolds.

Caleb turns his head to the side to see her and simply nods "Yes", indicating that he understands. He takes in the sight of Mrs. Doyle's pretty eyes intently staring and scoping out his ass for her next assault. Once again, she has that cute, sexy, smirk on her face that tells him she's really enjoying the view of his body, as well as, administering this discipline. He watches as she gently taps the strap twice on his cheeks, then changes her smiley smirk to that stern, sexy, "I'm gonna stripe your butt good" type of look. Her eyebrows come closer together with this slightly angry look as she raises the strap high and swings.

<CRACK><SMACK><CRACK>

Mrs. Doyle delivers several relentless swats that actually makes Caleb get out of the bent over position and bounce in place. His dick is still completely hard and pointing straight up toward the ceiling. Mrs. Doyle gets another eyeful of his beautiful penis bouncing up and down right in front of her, as Caleb moves his hands behind him to clutch and rub his butt. This sight of his hot, athletic body bouncing that close in front of her is just too much for her to ignore. Her mind plays an image of her boldly reaching out with her left hand and cupping his testicles. The movie then has her giving them a medium squeeze as she moves her body close to the point where their lips are just about touching. She opens her mouth slightly and goes in for a sexy, passionate kiss as her tongue eagerly pushes through her full, red, lips. She quickly snaps out of this daydream and comes back to reality. Her big, blue eyes look directly into his as she sternly instructs.

"Get back in position!"

Mrs. Doyle maintains a tight grip on his left bicep as she escorts and pushes him back in place over the arm of the sofa. Once Caleb is back in place, she finally releases her grip, and without saying a word, delivers the last flurry with her strap.

Caleb impressively stays in position bent over the sofa as her leather strap adds more red stripes across his cheeks. He tries his best to stay silent but he can't help it as he gives way to the pain and responds.

"YEOW!... OUCH!"

Mrs. Doyle is feeling more than satisfied with the strapping she just delivered, puts it down and once again takes hold of his muscular arm.

"Let's go... walk this hiney to the bathroom." She commands.

Chapter 12

Caleb doesn't hesitate and immediately walks to the bathroom as Mrs. Doyle follows alongside him. Her eyes took in the beautiful view of his striped cheeks with every step. Caleb's rear-end resembles the American flag, with a good number of bright red stripes going across it.

Once they both enter the bathroom, Mrs. Doyle leads him over the sink. Caleb looks at his reflection in the bathroom mirror as Mrs. Doyle lathers a bar of soap in her hands.

"I told you that I also washed Dillon's mouth out with soap yesterday. Let this be a lesson to you since you told me how your mouth often gets you in trouble." She commands, "Open!"

Mrs. Doyle takes the soap and thoroughly rubs it all over Caleb's tongue. She's turned on beyond belief as the wetness from her vagina is now trickling down the inside of her leg. She continues to take in the full view of Caleb's amazing body as he's totally naked and now bent over her bathroom sink.

His cute ass is way too hot for her to ignore and she opens her hand and delivers a hard slap onto his right cheek. She loves feeling his skin so much that she delivers another slap to his left cheek.

Caleb doesn't make a sound as her hand slaps fail in comparison to the pain he already felt with her strap. Mrs. Doyle's hands are itching to feel more of his tight ass as she continues and now applies a flurry of hand slaps.

She then takes her left hand, and with a forceful pinching motion, she grabs a good amount of his right butt cheek. She holds it tight and continues pinching him as hard as she can as her right hand navigates the bar of soap all throughout Caleb's mouth. She makes sure to fully cover every inch of his tongue and once she's finally satisfied, she gives the command for him to spit it out and rinse.

Caleb did the best he could to try and remain silent, but now he really feels the force of her pinching his ass, and responds.

"OOoouch!"

His response definitely satisfied Mrs. Doyle, as a mission accomplished type of smirk, comes across her face.

"Okay Caleb, let's go! Move it… into Dillon's room."
"On the bed… lie on your back… hands at your side." Mrs. Doyle once again spews commands.

Caleb follows her orders and lies flat on his back with his hands at his side. He is on full display with his super erect penis extending past his belly button. He watches her leave the room only to return in less then a minute holding a wooden spoon.

"This is the final part of your spanking," she informed him.

Mrs. Doyle stands over him and looks directly down at his huge hard on. Little does Caleb know what's going on in her mind as her eyes take in every inch of him. She's doing all she could not to grab his beautiful, young cock and suck him into oblivion. There's another little voice in her head that's telling her to just hop aboard, ride him, and fuck his brains out.

Mrs. Doyle refrains from both of these temptations and proceeds to carry out the discipline she promised him. She reaches down and tightly grabs hold of his ankles. She then pulls his legs upward and firmly tucks them under her left armpit. Caleb suddenly recalls her son Ryder telling him about this spanking position yesterday. This is one of the positions that his mom spanked him in with Mrs. Beck watching for that baseball through the window incident.

He's doing all he can not to explode and shoot his sperm everywhere as Mrs. Doyle takes control and handles his body. His eyes follow her every move as he sees and feels his legs become firmly tucked under her left armpit. Caleb couldn't help but notice, that once again, she had that same little smiley type of smirk on her face as her eyes stared with intensity at his rear-end.

Once she has his legs exactly where she wants them, she gives his body a quick little turn to the left. This exposes his sit spot and that delicate area right underneath the butt cheeks where the tops of the legs meet. He then watches as her "smiley" expression changes to a "time to do my job" type of look. For Caleb, he finds this stern look of sheer determination that Mrs. Doyle is wearing on her face incredibly sexy. This stern, strict side of hers is such a huge contrast to her sweet, loving personality that it actually turns him on.. Big Time!

Once again, Mrs. Doyle gets that vertical furrow between her eyebrows, as she tightens her jaw and purses her lips tightly together. He looks on as she raises the wooden spoon high in the air and proceeds to deliver one spank after another in a fast, hard flurry that completely adds a deeper shade of red to this entire area of his backside.

<SMACK><SMACK><SMACK><CRACK><CRACK><SMACK><SMACK>

Caleb tries his best to hold it in, but he just can't keep his silence. She's really giving it to him good with the wooden spoon and he responds with a resounding, "Ow… Ouch… Oh!"

As Caleb's body starts shaking from the pain, Mrs. Doyle tightens her grip around his legs. She doesn't let up just yet. Instead, she gives one final inspection of his rear-end to make sure she didn't miss a spot. With that fierce look still planted on her face, she continues and finishes him off with one last flurry of relentless swats.

Mrs. Doyle hears Caleb's response to her spanking as music to her ears. She's now totally convinced that Caleb will always remember her... remember this, his first spanking, for the rest of his life.

She takes a moment to admire her work and takes in the full view of Caleb's completely reddened bottom. There is not a single patch of white skin left on his entire hiney. Mrs. Doyle really went to town on him and she knows that this was the hardest spanking that she's ever given… period.

She places the spoon on the bed and lets go of Caleb's legs. She watches as he immediately turns onto his side in a semi-fetal position. His hands are clenching and rubbing his bottom in an effort to ease the pain.

"Your discipline is over, Caleb." She tells him.
"I want you to get dressed and go home to think about this."
"I'll come over to check on you later and we'll have a follow-up conversation."

Chapter 13

Caleb stands up to face her as his hands remain glued to his ass cheeks, continuing to rub them vigorously. Mrs. Doyle turns him around and takes one last look at his glowing, red bottom. It's totally bright red with strap marks, as well as, wooden spoon imprints all over it.

"It's safe to say that hiney of yours is going to be sore for a few days, my dear."
"You wanted to experience a serious spanking and that's exactly what you got." She confirmed with that cute smirk of hers.

"Thank you, Ma'am. I will never forget this." He tells her.

Mrs. Doyle responds, "Caleb, I'm going to hold you accountable for your grades when you go back for night classes to get your bachelors degree. Plus, you can always come to me if you feel that you are getting off track... deal?"

"You're saying that you'll spank me again?" Caleb asked, "If I need it? Or don't get good grades?"

"In a heartbeat!" Mrs. Doyle smirks, "and no one has to know."

"I totally need that structure and accountability." Caleb replies, "Thank you, Mrs. Doyle... That means a lot. I won't ever forget this... Can I give you a hug?"

"Of course, honey." Mrs. Doyle extends her arms wide open and embraces him.

She couldn't help but feel his stiff penis rubbing against her leg. She easily feels every inch of it so much, that it's as if she wasn't wearing a sundress at all.

"Oh and Caleb..." She mentions as they end their embrace.

"That is absolutely beautiful." She pointed directly to his totally erect penis.

"You need to go home and take care of yourself." She smirks.

Caleb is truly embarrassed but manages to give her a gentle smile as he goes and retrieves his clothes. Once completely dressed, he exits her house, walks across the lawn, and quickly retreats to the comfort of his own bedroom. This moment couldn't come fast enough as Caleb lies on his bed, pulls his pants down, grabs hold of his cock, and starts vigorously stroking himself. He closes his eyes and visions of Mrs. Doyle takes over and floods his mind. Not only with the way she just spanked him, but he's also picturing kissing and touching her in a romantic way. He then pictures turning the tables and getting rough with her. He would love to get at her plump, pumpkin-shaped ass, and do all kinds of things to it!

With those images flooding his mind, it took all of 30 seconds before he let out an exasperated moan with sperm shooting all over his washboard abs. After his orgasm is complete, he takes a moment to clean himself off and then lies back down. It's a lot to process for anyone, let alone a 22 year-old, hormone gone crazy, guy.

In the meantime, back at Mrs. Doyle's house, she already has her panties down around her ankles. She's so turned on that she immediately grabbed her vibrator and is pleasuring herself in her bedroom. She can't help but replay the visions of aggressively handling Caleb and stripping him down to his birthday suit. Visions of that super fine ass of his and that absolutely beautiful, rock-hard cock were filling her mind. It takes less than a minute for her to explode into an epic orgasm that has her body shaking with pleasure. Disciplining her young stud of a neighbor is so much different than disciplining her own kids. It actually turned her on so much that her vagina was dying for attention. Her adrenaline was completely revved up to the point where she didn't want to stop delivering her strap to his bare ass. She also did all she could to withdraw from climbing aboard, riding his cock, and fucking his brains out.

As she lays in bed, she fantasizes and contemplates about the next time when she will have the opportunity to punish him. She also hopes that he takes her up on the offer to get the physical exam that is required for his new job from her. There is no doubt that Megan Doyle is infatuated and now fantasizing about Caleb as much as he is about her.

Chapter 14

About an hour and a half goes by as Caleb anticipates Mrs. Doyle stopping over to check on him. Many thoughts are going thru his young mind as his rear end is still feeling the after effects of her disciplining. Just then, a knock on the door interrupts the movie his head was re-playing. He walks over to his front door and welcomes her inside.

"Hi, Mrs. Doyle… Come on in." He greets her with his amazing smile.

"Thank you, honey." She replies and enters.

Caleb motions for them to sit down in the living room. As she walks over to the sofa, his eyes instantly take in the view of her curvy hips and that beautiful, ample bottom of hers hidden beneath her baggy lounge pants. Of course, she smells amazing as her skin gives off the scent of a fresh shower.

"So, I know this is quite different, but I always check on my kids an hour or so after I spank them. This is when we talk calmly and I explain my reasons for disciplining them. I also make sure they fully understand their actions and the consequences of their misbehavior." She relays.

"That's so loving and caring… You are an amazing mom." Caleb replies.

Mrs. Doyle reveals her pearly white teeth as she smiles from ear to ear over Caleb's nice words.

"Well, it's the right thing to do after reddening their bottoms." She jokes.

Caleb chuckles along as he becomes even more in awe of his next-door neighbor. Her maturity and the way she speaks and handles herself are so different than girls his age. It's no wonder that his good friend Ryder talks this way about his mom. Caleb is seeing firsthand that she's exactly as Ryder explained to him yesterday. She's an amazing woman and a caring mom that possesses an abundance of nurturing and loving qualities, along with a strong, stern side that is displayed only when necessary.

Mrs. Doyle looks at Caleb with sincerity in her eyes as she takes his hand and gently holds it.

"Caleb, I hope this experience and the way I disciplined you was exactly the way you needed it to be. You were so clear and concise that I was beyond impressed with the way you relayed your needs to me. As I mentioned to you, it seemed so similar to my own experience with my college professor when I was your age. I couldn't get him out of my mind and I just craved and needed him to spank me." She reiterates.

"It was exactly what I needed." Caleb responds, "I wanted to experience the way you discipline Ryder and Dillon. I will never forget it, Ma'am. Thank you so much. I really need this structure and accountability in my life and you're the perfect person to keep me in line."

Mrs. Doyle gets a slightly embarrassed and concerned look in her eyes as she responds.

"Well, you're very welcome, sweetheart. You can count on me to keep you in line. I will hold you accountable for your work ethic and school grades, as well as, anything else that you want me to. You can even come to me whenever you feel that you need to. All I ask is that we just keep this between ourselves. There is no need for my husband, my sons, or anyone else to know that I discipline you." Mrs. Doyle continues, "Is that agreeable?"

"Absolutely! You have my word, Ma'am." Caleb responds without hesitation, "I respect you more than you know and you can trust me with our secret."

"Caleb, I do need to apologize to you." Mrs. Doyle adds, "You asked to be disciplined the same way as I handled Dillon yesterday, and I did to some extent. However, I got carried away and I really gave it to you... hard! Actually, it was the hardest spanking that I ever gave anyone and it may have even been too much for your needs. You are one attractive young man and that body of yours is insane! I couldn't stop focusing on your hiney. It's just so cute and perfect for spanking!"

The two of them laugh together at her admittance and her humor as Mrs. Doyle continues to express her thoughts.

"So please accept my apology for spanking you that severely." She concluded with a look of concern.

Caleb continues to hold her hand in an understanding type of way as his big, green eyes stare intently into hers. Of course, all he is thinking about right now is kissing her beautiful lips. He'd never been with a girl older than 24 in his life, but in this moment, Mrs. Doyle is all he's craving. It seems they've already formed a genuine and unique bond of total trust and respect. I mean, she just stripped every stitch of clothing off his body and vowed not to tell anyone. Caleb takes a moment to gather his thoughts and responds.

"Mrs. Doyle, thank you for the apology and the compliments. I can assure you that it was perfect. Yes, it was intense, but I needed my first spanking to be like that. The truth is, that I've been thinking about this and about you spanking me non-stop since yesterday. I wanted you to spank me hard and I'm sure you realized from my erection, that I was incredibly turned on. This was building up inside of me and I was so worried that I was going to explode with my sperm shooting everywhere. So, it's me that needs to apologize for having a hard-on."

Once again, Mrs. Doyle is thoroughly impressed by Caleb. The way he chooses his words and expresses his feelings are way beyond the years of a 22-year-old. Megan Doyle knows that he's already stirred up some feelings inside of her that have been dormant for years during her 20-plus years of marriage. She also knows that this agreement is flat out wrong, but there is no way she wants to stop it.

"Caleb, there is definitely no need for you to apologize. You've been 100% honest about your desires and everything that you were feeling. I can tell you, that as a nurse, I've seen it all," she giggles and carries on.

"I've had patients get erections during my examinations... I've even had women get turned on... So, it's okay... I understand... The body does what it wants to do!" She adds.

"Thanks for understanding," Caleb replies, "It makes me feel a little better, although I'm still quite embarrassed about it. Since we're being completely honest and open, I did come home and take care of it as you suggested."

He shakes his head in disbelief, "I really can't believe that I'm having this conversation with you... After all, you're my good friend's mom, and my next door neighbor... It's so crazy!"

Mrs. Doyle chuckles and chimes in, "Yeah, I know... It is crazy, but I'm really glad that we've established such an open communication and level of trust. It's nice to know that we can talk about these personal things. So, I guess it's only fair for me to come clean also."

She looks at him with that gorgeous smile of hers, "I had to relieve myself as well... twice! I was extremely turned on by seeing you naked and handling you, Caleb. I never expected it to affect and excite me as much as it did."

Now it's Mrs. Doyle who's fighting every urge to kiss him and climb all over him.

Caleb smiles as he feels a huge sense of relief hearing that Mrs. Doyle was turned from disciplining him as well. He had that thought several times throughout his punishment and now she just confirmed it. He knew it was a dead giveaway when that cute smile and sexy smirk lit up her face the moment she pulled down his pants and administered the leather strap to his rear end. He then continued to see it several times throughout his punishment. It's refreshing to know that Mrs. Doyle enjoyed spanking him just as much as he enjoyed having her spank him.

Caleb volunteers, "The craziest thing is, spanking was never even on my radar until I saw you give your son that spanking yesterday. Now, I feel it will always be a part of my life. So it's all because of you." He concludes with a laugh.

"Well, I'm not sure if that's a good thing or not." Mrs. Doyle laughs and responds, "As I have told you, I've really been into spanking ever since college. I craved it, needed it, and I loved getting handled aggressively. There's an entire side to my sexuality that's been ignored for years. Jim doesn't have it in him."

She continues, "I would love to bring BDSM, spanking, toys, role-plays into my life with someone that I'm drawn to, but I really don't want to cheat on my husband. I would have tied him up and spanked him years ago, but I know it's not his thing… So, until now, spanking wasn't a sexual part of my life. I've just been a mom that spanked her kids for misbehaving. Aside from them, I've never done that to anyone else but you," she laughs, "I'm afraid you ruined me, Caleb. I might want to give up nursing and become a professional dominatrix!"

"I'd be your best customer!" Caleb quickly chimed, "Actually, we can open up a side business. I would have no problem putting naughty girls in their place!"

"Oh God!" She blushes, "I'm going to need my vibrator when I get home. You're turning me on… AGAIN!"

"So, it sounds like spanking will play a part in the bedroom and in your sex life… Am I right?" She comes right out and asks him.

"Funny you should ask," he replied, "It sure will… I've already watched so many videos of everything from BDSM, bondage, blindfolds, to using sex toys and YES… even role playing. I actually

went to the adult store last night and purchased a few things…
Needless to say, I'll be more open, creative, and hopefully even
better in the bedroom."

"Oh my God… You're killing me, Caleb," Mrs. Doyle laughs,
"Sounds like you went all in. There are gonna be some really lucky
girls when you get done with them!"

Right now, she's about as close as she can get to his face without
having their lips touch. She's fighting every urge to jump his bones.

She gives him that sexy smirk of hers, and giggles, "Care to show
me what you bought?"

Chapter 15

Caleb retrieves the gym bag from his bedroom closet and shows her all the kinky toys that he just purchased. He pulls them out one at a time.

"Here they are... handcuffs, a blindfold, rope, a riding crop, a wooden paddle," He continues with the sexy show and tell.

"Check this out," he says, "a strap just like yours!"

Mrs. Doyle comments, "Mmmhmm."

He continues, "Here's some edible massage oil that heats up, and these..."

He pulls out a couple of vibrators, anal beads, a butt plug, and a strap on harness.

"HOLY MOLY!" Mrs. Doyle reacts, "You weren't kidding. It looks like you bought the whole store!"

They both giggle together like two grammar school kids. There is such an easy-going vibe between them when they talk about anything sexual in nature, that you'd never even think that Caleb was half her age... You also would never guess that before today their conversations were only very neighborly, like the common, "hi, how are you?", and on the surface level. Other than Marcy Beck, she never talks this openly with anyone else about anything sexual. Definitely not her vanilla husband.

Mrs. Doyle is beyond impressed as Caleb continues to really capture her attention and her heart. Of course, she can't seem to get his insane body off her mind, but it goes deeper than that, and even more dangerous. For some reason, right now, she's all giddy, with that love-struck feeling over the young heartthrob. Caleb may be young, but he has this incredible maturity to him. So far, he's crystal clear about what he wants, and he hasn't held back in explaining everything that he's feeling. That's the reason why, right now, his rear-end looks like it went through World War 1!

Mrs. Doyle grabs the strap-on harness and looks it over. Her mind contemplates saying something but then she goes silent. Finally, she gets the nerve and asks him.

"I hate to ask this Caleb, and you don't have to answer." She continues, "Are you gay or bi-sexual?"

"No… Not at all." Caleb laughed out loud and quickly responded, "Just because I bought a strap-on?"

"Well... Yeah, I guess that made me wonder," she replied with honesty.

"No, I plan on using that on a girl, at the same time as intercourse. You know… double penetration," he answered.

"Oh Yummy!" Mrs. Doyle commented as that flustered look came over her again.

Caleb didn't stop there, and continued, "I would also be open to have a girl use it on me. I love it when a girl does anal play on me," he nervously admitted.

Mrs. Doyle clears her throat, not really knowing what to say about that. She's a huge fan of everything anal, but again, has kept this side of her buried deep. She then makes sure he understands and explains, "I love all that, but I haven't had anything kinky like that since my college days. I mean… when Mr. Doyle and I first met… yeah, we had great sex. That's the reason we got married. I became pregnant with Ryder at 24 years old, just when I started my first job as a nurse."

Mrs. Doyle really opens up, "It's not like I don't love Jim. It's just that I never had that fire, that passion for him. He's a great dad, and he totally supported me while I went back to college. I really wanted to become a doctor, but then… Whammo!... hurricane Dillon… that wasn't planned either!"

Caleb senses this is a sensitive subject for her and he says nothing but just listens.

"So, needless to say, Jim only used a few vibrators on me, but nothing like what you purchased," she admits, "he's definitely not that kinky."

She laughs and continues, "and I never used any of them on him. I, on the other hand, have a very kinky nature. I would be open to using so many toys, but he's just not into that. So this huge part of me became stifled and then I just forgot about it… Until now, with you!"

"I see… how about spanking?" Caleb asks. "He never spanked you?"

"No, just a slap on the ass here and there during sex. It was nothing like the way I give it. It was only with his hand and it wasn't even that hard. He just doesn't have it in him… I kinda wish he did." Mrs. Doyle tells him.

Caleb's young mind instantly creates a video of him completely dominating Mrs. Doyle and giving her the same type of spanking that she just gave him. Just then, his phone rings, and Mrs. Doyle gives him the nod that it's okay for him to answer it.

She hears the voice of a younger girl telling Caleb that she'll pick up some dinner for them and she'll be over in an hour or so. The conversation ends and Caleb apologizes to Mrs. Doyle for the interruption.

"Don't be silly, sweetheart." She tells him, "I heard she's coming over… Just remember that your butt is marked to smithereens and if she sees it, she'll want some explanations."

Caleb responds, "No worries, I already have it all planned… that's where the blindfold and handcuffs come into play… Just so you know, I'm serious about our promise to each other… I won't tell anyone… You can trust me."

"Clever… and kinky… I love it!" Mrs. Doyle commented, "So what's her name?"

"Sarah," Caleb replied.

"I bet you'll make her smile for a while." Mrs. Doyle laughs at her own humor.

"Excuse me?" Caleb asks, not knowing what the joke was.

"Oh, that was just me showing my age… That was a line from an old song by Hall & Oats, called Sarah Smile." She explains in embarrassment and continues, "Well, I'm gonna leave you. Have fun tonight. You'll have to let me know how those new toys work. I think I'll do some website searches myself tonight." She added and gave him a little wink.

"Since you're home alone, I'll text you some of the websites and videos that I watched, especially the ones that have spankings. There are some really, really hot ones!" Caleb tells her, "Just remember to delete my text from your phone."

"Will do!" Mrs. Doyle responds, "Go easy on her. I can't wait to hear how it goes." She giggles as she walks out the door and heads back to her home.

Her head is spinning and her mind is complete mush after that conversation with Caleb. She realizes that she's even more into him now that they shared an emotional connection as well. Her phone chimes with a text from Caleb of several kinky websites and videos for her to check out.

She glances at the message, opens the door to her house, and heads straight for her computer. She gets that sexy smirk on her face that says it all. She can't wait to dive in and get reacquainted to the exciting world of kink that she's been missing for so long.

Chapter 16

It's been just over an hour since Mrs. Doyle left and Caleb still has her on his mind. Thankfully, he remembers and deletes the text that he recently sent to his pretty neighbor of the kinky websites and videos. The doorbell rings as he walks over and opens the door.

"Hi Babe!" Sarah enters and plants a sexy kiss on Caleb, "God, I missed you."

"Hey beautiful, I missed you too!" Caleb replies, "You look stunning!"

Sarah is rocking a white baby doll blouse and a pair of tight jeans that show off her super toned legs and perfect bubble butt. Her tanned skin and dark brown hair make her smile even more radiant. She's a stunning beauty that can definitely match and may even surpass Caleb's athletic ability. Especially since she's the star of the college softball team. Caleb will be the first to admit that she's in better shape and that her workouts are even more intense than his. He takes in all of her beauty as her big brown eyes stare into his.

"You hungry?" She asks, "I picked up some dinner."

"A little, but I can wait," Caleb answered.

"Good, cause I want to fuck your brains out!" Sarah boldly replies as her lips passionately go straight to his neck. After the soft, tender, kiss on his neck, she moves her lips upwards and gives his earlobe a sexy, little bite. Then she allows her hands to slip under his t-shirt and starts lifting it off his body.

"Not so fast, sexy girl." He stops her, "Tonight you're all mine and you're gonna listen and obey my every command... Got it?"

"Oooh! I like that!" She doesn't hesitate and excitedly answers.

"Close your eyes." Caleb instructs as he leads her against his living room wall.

He turns her body so she's facing the wall with her adorable ass out. He retrieves his gym bag and grabs the blindfold from inside of it.

"Keep those eyes closed, baby." He instructs as he secures it in place over her eyes.

He then lifts her shirt off over her head and completely removes it from her body. He unsnaps her lace bra and throws it on the floor as his hands reach around her and cup her small, but perfectly round, breasts. He kisses her neck as her head tilts backward to accept his lips on her skin. His fingers give each nipple a little pinch as his lips slid down to kiss the back of her shoulders.

"Mmmmm! Oh My God, Babe… that feels so amazing!" She lets him know without hesitation about how good it feels.

Caleb continues to kiss the back of her shoulders and then lets his tongue lick all the way down her spine until it meets the top of her jeans.

"Ooh! Mmmm..." She instantly replies.

He then spins her around so she's facing him as he reaches into his bag of tricks and goes for the edible massage oil. The blindfold takes away her knowing and anticipating what is about to happen. Caleb's hands run a generous amount of the cherry almond-scented oil onto her perky breasts. The slower calculated pace coupled with the blindfold and Caleb's willingness to take charge, make this adventure super erotic for her.

Sarah has no idea what he's about to do next and she's so turned on that it's sending shivers up and down her spine. Caleb dabs more of the oil onto her nipples as he rubs with just the right amount of pressure. He then engulfs her left breast with his entire mouth as he toggles between giving some gentle kisses and cute little sucks to her strawberry-shaped nipples. As his lips come off her skin, he blows on the area over her nipples where the massage oil was generously applied.

Sarah feels the oil heat up and loves the sensation that it's creating on her skin. She instantly responds with her approval.

"Ahh!"

Her breathing increases along with her heartbeat as Caleb continues to rock her world. He repeats the exact same pattern on her right breast as he kisses and then sucks a little harder, ending it with a cute nibble this time. He's thoroughly enjoying the taste of the cherry almond oil coupled with his girlfriend's skin as he once again blows to create heat, then licks all over her entire breast. He then equally divides his kisses and licks over each breast as her nipples instantly respond and pop out even more.

"Oh My God! That feels amazing!" She couldn't help but repeat that exact phrase again as her hands grabbed the back of his head.

Caleb is feeling more confident and more sexy as ever as he continues to blow his girlfriend's mind. The new approach and the added toys so far are a welcome addition. Usually they just go at it like animals and fuck until they drop, which isn't a bad thing, but now to have this type of foreplay in addition might just be the golden ticket... And Caleb's just getting started!

He continues to apply more oil to her luscious tits and downward to her flat, well toned stomach. His tongue traces downward and licks over her belly button and onto the sides of her waist, right above her jeans. He kisses and blows on these areas, making her skin heat up in response. Sarah feels the warmth of the oil penetrating her and once again starts breathing heavily.

Caleb kisses and licks just below her bellybutton as his right hand reaches down over her jeans and rubs her vagina. His slow, methodical approach is teasing her beyond belief as she wiggles in place from the sensations she's feeling.

"Feeling good?" He asks and thoughtfully checks in with her.

"It's fucking amazing… You're fucking amazing!" She replies slightly out of breath, "I'm so wet… So turned on, baby. Let me get at that dick of yours!"

"No, tonight you're under my command. I'm dictating your every move and I'm just getting started." Caleb replies, "I want you to communicate with me every step of the way. Let me know how everything feels and most importantly, give me a heads up if you feel close to orgasm. Got It?"

"Yes, Babe." She confirmed.

Caleb double checks and waves his hands over her face to make sure the blindfold is still in place. There is no doubt that she's unable to see anything as she doesn't flinch or move an inch. He reaches into his bag and pulls out the handcuffs. He quickly slides them onto her wrists, closes them, and places the key in his pocket. Sarah is a bit startled as she feels the handcuffs lock around her wrists and limit her arm mobility.

"Now the fun really starts." He announced with a sarcastic grin on his face.

Chapter 17

Caleb looks at the beautiful sight right before his eyes. He has his girlfriend naked from the waist up with oil over her breast and torso. Her skin is glowing like a beacon as he now focuses his attention on removing those amazing jeans.

He reaches down and unsnaps the top button around her waist. He starts to pull the tight jeans down and gives her a little tap on the hips which instructs her to wiggle to make his job easier. Sarah follows his lead as she wiggles her cute hips while he gives a forceful tug and makes them fall down to her ankles. He removes her shoes, then taps on each foot, signaling for her to fully step out of the jeans. Sarah obeys and is left standing in her pretty, laced, thong panties.

Caleb reaches into his bag and grabs a long beige rope. He secures it around the handcuffs and walks Sarah to a nice clear area in the middle of his living room. He throws the end of the rope over an exposed beam of his cathedral ceiling and pulls it until Sarah's arms are totally extended upward. Once he has her in the perfect position, he loops it several times and ties it around her wrists. This is a bold move for him to make on her and he wonders if she is going to be scared and freak out.

Even though they love fucking each other, they've only been together for a month. He knows Sarah's complete relationship history, and though she wasn't a virgin when he banged her, she's only had 2 other short-term boyfriends. She told him all about her sexual experiences, which haven't been a lot at all. In fact, it's safe to say that Caleb and her fucked 10 times more in this month, when they got together, than she had with both her past boyfriends. Needless to say, Sarah is still learning about her body and may not even know where her G-spot really is.

Caleb takes a step back to admire the way she looks tied with her arms overhead, positioned in the center of the room with just a thong on her body. He walks around the 20-year-old beauty, and stalks her like an animal about to devour its prey. She has no idea if he's in front of her, behind her, or even near her. She feels a combination of excitement and a bit of fear, not knowing what will come next.

Caleb quietly kneels down in front of her and waits for at least a minute to build up the tension. The silence and complete stop of action has Sarah totally confused and guessing as she's tied-up and helpless. Caleb taps the screen of his cell phone which sends music across the Bluetooth speakers in the room. The silence gives way as he slowly increases the volume until his living room is flooded with hypnotic beats and sexy music.

He lets another minute of inactivity go by before he flattens his tongue and places it on her left ankle. He gives it several sexy kisses and then licks and traces all the way up her inner thigh and stopping just short of where her panties cover her vagina. Sarah trembles and gasps as she feels his tongue explore this area of her body. She lets out some sexy moans that let Caleb know that everything he's doing is totally pleasing to her. He continues to let his tongue strategically lick all around her panties to thoroughly tease her. Caleb then guides his lips around her left hip and spins her around so her perfect bubble butt is out and facing him. His tongue explores every inch of her left butt cheek as his hands squeeze and grope every part of her amazing ass.

"Aahh… Mmm..." Sarah blurts out as his tongue wanders down her butt and tickles the area of her inner thigh close to her labia.

"Fuck… That feels so good, baby!" She says loud enough for him to hear over the music.

Caleb reaches for more oil and rubs it all over her basketball-shaped butt and super toned legs. He then backs away and turns the music up even louder to further diminish her sense of hearing. Sarah's mind continues to wonder and tries to anticipate what his next move will be as she remains handcuffed, tied, and helpless. The blindfold totally eliminates her sense of sight and now the loud hypnotic music did the same to her sense of hearing. After a couple minutes of inactivity, Caleb surprises her and places his entire mouth over her left ear. He breathes into her ear canal and whispers in a sexy voice.

"Stick out your tongue, baby."

Sarah obeys as her tongue pushes through her beautiful, plump lips. Caleb licks his tongue over her perky breasts once again and then places his tongue onto hers. He holds her face gently with his left hand as his right hand reaches back, grabs a small amount of her hair, and gives it a little tug. He kisses her with a fiery amount of passion unlike he's ever kissed her before.

Sarah's sense of taste gets awakened as her tongue discovers the flavor of the cherry almond oil that's all over Caleb's tongue. The kiss they are sharing goes on for several minutes as his tongue explores every inch of her luscious mouth. It's as sexy and as passionate as can be and is a thing of beauty that just about anyone would pay to see, especially from this incredibly hot, young couple. Sarah feels the wetness accumulating in her vagina as she's totally turned on by everything that Caleb is doing to her. She loves feeling the softness of his kiss mixed with the firm tug of her hair being pulled. Once their kiss finally ends, she lets out the sexiest moan Caleb's ever heard to date.

"Oooh… Mmmmm… Aaah" Fills the living room as the wetness flows from her vagina and starts to moisten her lace panties.

"I want you so bad!" She calls out in a totally out of breath voice.

Caleb's dick is back to being as hard and as solid as a baseball bat as he continues to totally dominate his girlfriend. Who would have thought that seeing Mrs. Doyle spank her son would be the catalyst for all these new ideas that he's using. It's amazing how much he's learned in the last 24 hours from watching endless spanking and kinky BDSM videos.

He drops back down to his knees, leaving Sarah wondering where his lips went off to. That question is quickly answered as she feels his lips kiss the fleshiest part of her ass where the back of her thighs and butt meet. He flattens his tongue and licks every inch of this under butt area and then blows on it to activate the heat of the massage oil. Sarah feels her sit spot area heat up and once again lets out an incredibly sexy moan.

"Aaah!"

This is music to Caleb's ears as he continues to lick every inch of her booty and then ends it with a cute, little bite on her right butt cheek. The sudden shock of pain is a complete contrast to the pleasure as it takes Sarah by surprise. She more than approves of this new sensation and lets him know.

"Ouch… Oh, God Yes!" She responds.

Caleb's dick responds and gets even more erect as it pops through the top of his jeans. He grabs the waistband of her lace thong and yanks it down with force to her ankles before completely removing it and tossing it across the room. Sarah squirms a little in place as she experiences the feeling of total vulnerability from having her last piece of clothing removed.

Caleb remains kneeling with her ass at eye level to him. He grabs and forcefully spreads her cheeks as his tongue licks the crack of her ass and then explores and rims her rectum. He alternates between licking and kissing, and then sucks and pulls a small amount of her flesh thru his mouth, ending with another sexy, little bite. Sarah more than approves and responds loudly over the music.

"Ahh! Fuck Yes!… That feels insane!... You need to FUCK me baby!... I need that dick!"

"Wow! What language, Missy." Caleb responds, "I had no idea you were such a bad girl with a dirty mouth."

"I'm a good girl, baby... I just want to feel your dick in my pussy. I'm so fucking turned on… You're blowing my mind!… Fuck me… Fuck me HARD!" Sarah responds.

Caleb stands and reaches for his newly acquired black riding crop. Without her sense of sight, Sarah has no idea what's coming next.

"Tonight, I WANT you to be a bad girl." Caleb emphasizes, "I want you to be really bad and tell me once again what you want… AND this time say it LOUDER!"

"I WANT THAT DICK OF YOURS! FUCK ME… MAKE ME CUM!... FUCK MY BRAINS OUT!" Sarah quickly yells out.

"Are you my bad girl?" Caleb asks.

"YES, I'm A BAD GIRL! I'm so FUCKING BAD! I need to be FUCKED like a bad girl!" She replies.

Caleb looks down at her beautiful, oily, glowing ass and hears her response. He raises the riding crop and takes aim.

"That's just what I wanted to hear!" He confirmed as he swings with a medium amount of force.

<CRACK>

Sarah feels the sting of the crop light up her right ass cheek and yelps.

"OUCH!"

"Didn't you know?… I love bad girls!" Caleb says in a sexy, sarcastic voice as he delivers another slightly harder dose of the crop to her left cheek.

<CRACK>

"YEOOUCH!" Sarah immediately responds as her left leg lifts up and comes off the floor.

Caleb's eyes take in the sight of her lovely ass getting painted with red crop marks. He's feeling extremely confident even though it's the first time he's ever spanked anyone. Again, he thinks about Mrs. Doyle and the position he was in just a few hours ago with his ass getting tanned. He displays a devious smile on his face and raises the riding crop again. He waits for his girlfriend's leg to return to the floor and then follows through and swings.

"OOW!" Sarah yelps out again, "FUCK YES… I'm a bad girl!… I'm your bad girl!… Spank me baby!"

Her response from getting spanked and wanting more actually took Caleb by surprise. He walks around the front of her and kneels down. His hands grab her ass cheeks with force as he plunges his tongue deep into her pussy.

"Aahhhh! YES! YES!" The intensity is way too much for Sarah to remain composed as she feels his tongue lick and suck all over her clitoris, labia, and into her pussy.

"I'm close, Baby. I'm gonna cum!" She announces to him.

Caleb quickly pulls his mouth away to further tease and prolong her orgasm.

"You're not going to cum until I give you permission to cum!" He says in a stern voice as he now reaches for his thick, leather strap.

Chapter 18

Without warning, he delivers the strap with force and paints a bright stripe in the middle of her ass cheeks.

"OOOH!" Sarah immediately responds as she wiggles and dances in place from the sting.

"This ass is all mine. Do you know that?" Caleb sternly asks.

"Of course it is, baby!... It's all yours!" She replies.

Caleb taps the strap 3 times on her ass cheeks as he plans his next swat.

"Arch that ass out!" He instructs her.

Sarah immediately obeys and sticks her beautiful ass out to give him an easier target. Caleb pulls the strap back and delivers a hard, fluid swing.

This time it connects with the lower, sit spot region of her butt. Once again, she does a sexy wiggle and dances in place from the pain. She doesn't hold back and lets out a loud response.

"YEEOOW!"

Caleb walks around her in circles as his eyes take in all of his girlfriend's beauty. His dick is throbbing as he sees Sarah and all of her hotness handcuffed and blindfolded with her arms extended and tied upward with the rope.

He waves his hand in front of her face to make sure that she can't see a thing. Once again, she doesn't respond or even flinch. He positions himself over her right shoulder and places his mouth directly outside her ear canal. He gives a sexy little bite on her earlobe and then kisses her neck before returning to her ear.

"I'll ask you again," he says in a stern voice, "Are you a good girl or a bad girl?"

"I'm a bad girl that needs to be punished," she responds.

Her response actually surprises him as he was planning to show her his soft side. It's obvious that Sarah likes getting spanked or at least she likes it in this moment. He walks around her and looks down at her tight, round, perfect ass. It's accented with several crop marks and a couple of thick, bright red stripes from the strap.

"I had no idea you liked to be spanked, baby." Caleb whispers as he returns his mouth to her ear.

"I had no idea either. It's my first time being spanked," she replies, "I had no idea that you had this in you...but it's so FUCKING HOT... More... I want MORE!"

"Your safe word is RED... If anything gets too much, use that word and everything stops," he tells her.

Sarah shakes her head "Yes" and acknowledges that she understands. She willingly arches her back out without Caleb instructing her, preparing herself and anticipating getting another dose of the leather strap.

Caleb tip-toes away from her and dips into his bag of tricks for some more items. He quietly places them on the floor next to her as he returns and stands to her left side. She has no idea where her sexy boyfriend is until his voice gives a command.

"Spread those legs... Arch that ass out further!"

Sarah follows his orders. She spreads her legs as far as possible and sticks her ass out even more. Caleb reaches down and grabs some more rope. He quickly ties it around her left ankle and then pulls it tight and secures it to a leg of a table across the room. He repeats the same procedure, forcing Sarah to stay tied in this standing, spread eagle position. He picks up the leather strap, and without any warning, swings it very hard.

<CRACK>

It lands slightly more on her right butt cheek as the new red stripe indicates. Before Sarah can even respond, he swings again and directs his aim to her left cheek.

"OOOuch!... OOOh!" She begs, "FUCK... I want you so bad, baby... FUCK ME!

Her body wiggles and squirms, but since her legs are tied, they are unable to come off the floor. Caleb absolutely loves the sight of her squirming and trying to dance from his strap. Again he walks around and circles her like a shark ready to bite. The wetness from her vagina is now noticeably dripping down the inside of her thighs. Caleb smiles to himself and then he taps the strap lightly and takes aim. Once again, he doesn't hold back and swings it with force.

It lands dead center as another stripe appears across her rear end. Her voice responds loudly as her sexy body wiggles in place. Caleb quietly puts the strap down and plunges two fingers from his left hand deep into her pussy. Sarah was expecting another swat from the strap and is taken totally by surprise as she feels his fingers penetrate her and moans.

"OOOh!... YES!... Aaah!"

Her labored response is all he needs to hear as he continues to let his index and middle finger forcefully invade her. He takes his right hand, raises it high, and slaps her ass hard.

<SLAP><SLAP><SLAP>

Sarah continues to moan with pleasure as her ass has even more color from Caleb's hand prints.

He continues to finger her pussy as he kneels down in front of her and places his tongue on her clit. He alternates between flicking his tongue and sucking as he tastes every drop of her wetness.

"AAAh! FUCK YES!… I'm close!" She announces.

"CUM!" Caleb gives her the permission she was waiting for.

As he continues to finger and lick her pussy, he lets the index finger of his right hand plunge deep into her ass. Sarah now feels his finger enter her rectum and lets loose.

"AAAhh!…. GOD YES!… I'm cumming, baby!"

She explodes into an epic orgasm as her body trembles in place. Caleb holds all of his fingers deep in place and doesn't let up with his mouth until she's completely done shaking. His mouth gets a thorough taste of her every drop as her breathing deepens and then slowly returns to normal to let him know her orgasm is over.

He removes his finger from her ass, as well as, his fingers in her pussy and gives her a few final licks down the inside of her thighs as he pulls his mouth away from her vagina.

"Fuck baby!… Oh My God!" She quickly responds, "That was amazing!… I never… I'm lost for words."

"You're amazing, "Caleb whispers as he kisses her soft, pretty lips.

"I'm not sure what got you in the mood to spank me like that," Sarah tells him, "watching porn, reading magazines, but whatever it is… it's okay with me!"

Of course, Caleb doesn't admit to her that his next-door neighbor is the reason he's suddenly into spanking. He looks up to his girlfriend still blindfolded, handcuffed, and tied. Her skin is radiantly glistening from the combination of massage oil and sweat. He tenderly touches her face as his tongue enters her mouth, giving her a beautiful and sexy kiss. Sarah can taste herself on his tongue as once again their kiss extends for at least a minute or two. When it concludes, Sarah lets out a sexy moan and Caleb responds and says two words to her.

"My Turn!"

Chapter 19

He unties her legs and arms but leaves the handcuffs and blindfold on her. Caleb is a smart cookie and doesn't want to risk having Sarah see his ass, which is totally red and marked, from being disciplined a few hours ago by Mrs. Doyle.

"I want that dick, baby!" Sarah begs, "Take these off... Let me touch you, suck you, fuck you!"

"Oh, you're gonna get it, but tonight it's my way. The blindfold and handcuffs are staying on!" Caleb replies in a stern voice as he takes her hand and walks her over in the direction of his sofa. As he has her standing in place, he removes all of the pillows on the sofa and tosses them on the floor.

"I want to see you and touch you!" Sarah replies with a bit of an attitude as she reaches her hand downward to feel for his dick.

Caleb allows her hand to grab him and feel his huge erection through his jeans. He then unbuttons his jeans and pulls them down slightly below his butt, along with his underwear. He takes her hand and places it on his testicles before guiding it upward to let her feel the full extent of his erection.

"There... You felt it!" He replies, "Happy now?"

"Hell NO!" Sarah responds with more attitude as she drops to her knees and guides her tongue along the shaft of his penis.

Her handcuffed hands are clenched to his testicles as she opens her mouth and engulfs him.

"MMMmm, You taste amazing!" She tells him as her tongue does circles around the head of his penis.

"I want you so bad, Caleb."

She lets him know as her hands move upward and remove her blindfold. She gets a quick eyeful of her boyfriend's amazing dick.

"Mmmm... Yes... Now that's what I wanted to see!" She responds and quickly devours his dick in her mouth and starts sucking him with everything she's got.

"I told you this stays on!" Caleb sternly scolds her as he pulls away and places the blindfold back over her eyes.

He then reaches down and takes the long rope that's tied around the leg of the end table and wraps it several times, securing her arms around her waist. He ties it tightly to prevent her from having any arm mobility whatsoever.

"So, you really want to be a bad girl and disobey me tonight?" Caleb responds, "Fine, I'll show you exactly how I handle bad girls!"

Caleb yanks his pants and underwear back up and quickly sits on the sofa. Without wasting another second, he forcefully pulls Sarah over his lap. He places his right leg over her legs to prevent her from kicking and raising her legs. He raises his hand high and delivers a flurry of relentless slaps to her ass.

<SLAP><SLAP><SLAP><SLAP>

This time Sarah's response is much different as she quickly pleads and apologizes.

"OUCH! Okay, I'm sorry baby... Oow!"

Caleb doesn't hold back and administers several more to her already marked cheeks.

"OOOw! I apologize... You're in control, baby!" Sarah responds as her ass is ignited with his spanks.

Caleb pulls her up for a brief moment and then guides her into a different position. He takes a page out of Mrs. Doyle's spanking positions, escorting her onto the sofa, in a position where she's flat on her back. Sarah feels her body being handled and moved into position as her arms remain bound to her waist.

Caleb grabs hold of her ankles and lifts her legs up into the diaper position. He easily remembers how Mrs. Doyle had him in this exact position a few hours ago. Once he has Sarah's legs up in the air, he firmly tucks them under his left armpit. He gives her body a little twist to the left which automatically makes the sit spot region of her ass even more accessible.

Sarah remains motionless and is just putty in his hands as her body is maneuvered exactly where he wants it. Caleb raises his hand and administers a serious spanking.

<SLAP><SLAP><SLAP><SLAP><SLAP>

"OOOW!... OUCH!... OOOH!" Sarah instantly cries out.

"I told you, tonight it's my way!" Caleb scolds her as his hand rains down on her ass.

"YEOW!... I'm sorry babe!... OUCH! Sarah's loud cries and apology are easily heard over the glaring music.

Caleb doesn't hold back and really goes to town, making sure every last inch of her ass and upper legs are completely covered with his red hand prints.

<SLAP><SLAP><SLAP><SLAP>

"Oow!... I'm sorry!... Red!" Sarah uses her safe word.

Caleb instantly stops spanking her and releases her legs from his hold. He pulls her up with haste and bends her over the arm of the sofa. He quickly unbuttons his jeans and lowers them back down below his ass as he rams his dick with force into her pussy.

Sarah feels him penetrate her and thrust with force and her heavy breathing instantly returns. Caleb grabs a handful of her long, brown hair and holds onto it like he's riding a horse as he fucks her brains out with all the intensity he has. Sarah lets out moans of pleasure as her vagina is now flowing like a stream.

"Oooo!… Yes!... Oh God!… Yes!… Mmmmm!
"Fuck me, baby… Harder!…

Once again, Caleb takes her from pain to pleasure and thoroughly blows her mind as he continues to pound her hard, giving her exactly what she wanted. He feels all of her wetness as his huge dick rapidly and forcefully rams every inch of her pussy. It doesn't take long and he knows that he's close to exploding. He gives one final tug on her hair accompanied by a few hard thrusts before he pulls out of her and cums all over her lower back.

"Oh… Mmmm!" He moans with delight.

Sarah hears his moans and feels the warmth of his sperm on her skin. Just like a few minutes ago, she's totally turned on and as wet as can be.

"Give me all of it, baby!" She calls out as Caleb uses his hand and gives his dick some rapid strokes to make sure every drop of sperm comes out of his body. Once he's completely done, he lets out a resounding.

"Phew! That felt insane… Your pussy felt like heaven, baby!" He tells her as he grabs a towel and cleans his sperm off her lower back.

He knows Sarah is still turned on and completely wet as he grabs a vibrator from his toy bag. He pulls her up from the bent position over the sofa and once again lays her flat on her back. He spreads her legs and licks the wetness from the lips of her vagina. Sarah instantly responded.

"Mmmm!… Yes!… I'm gonna cum!"

Caleb turns the vibrator on and places it on the exact area of her clitoris that his lips are working. It's the first time he's used a vibrator on her, and he's taking his cues from all the kinky videos he's recently watched.

Sarah feels the magic as her entire body tingles. She wiggles her hips and gives a slight gyration to help navigate his lips exactly where she wants them. Caleb continues to let his tongue work it's magic along with the vibrator all over the sensitive areas of her labia and clit. He unties her arms, then unlocks and removes the handcuffs from her wrists. Right away Sarah instantly grabs the back of his head and holds him in place as she gyrates on his tongue. It doesn't take long as she erupts into another orgasm.

"Yes!... Right there, baby!... Aaah!... YES!" She lets him know as her entire body shakes vigorously.

Caleb waits for her body to completely stop shaking to make sure her orgasm is over before he pulls the vibrator and his tongue away. Then he quickly pulls his jeans and underwear back up and removes the blindfold from over her eyes. That last thing he wants is for her to see his red, marked-up ass as she regains her sense of sight.

"You totally blew my mind, baby!" She tells him, "That was freaking amazing... I'm speechless and spent!" She concludes with a laugh.

Her words along with the look in her eyes and the smile on her face, is all the proof that Caleb needed. The way he took control and dominated every fiber of her body has made his sexual confidence level rise to a new high in his young life.

Sarah looks around the room and sees the kinky toys that were used on her. Her eyes take in the vibrator, the massage oil, and then she focuses on the leather strap and the riding crop. She notices his gym bag, more rope, a wooden paddle, and a few other things that weren't even used next to it.

"Caleb, how the hell?… The kinky toys?… The blindfolds, rope?... The spanking?" Sarah can't quite fathom everything and remains lost for words and totally shocked at what just happened. She continues, "I had no idea that you were into this."

"BDSM? Spanking? When? How?" She asks, "I want to hear every detail." She tells him as she remains lying there in her birthday suit.

She looks at Caleb and eagerly waits for his response.

Chapter 20

"Well?" She asks him again as he fails to answer immediately.

"I'll tell you what... Let's clean up and have dinner and we'll continue this conversation. I'll tell you everything that you want to know, babe," Caleb responded.

"Can I see what else you have in your kinky bag over there?" She pointed across the room.

"No way!" He quickly responds, "There are still many surprises that I plan on doing to you and using in there."

Sarah laughs at his reply, then gives him a warm, loving hug.

"Like I said… I don't know what made you do that and be that aggressive, but I want more of it!" She tells him, "Okay, I need to take a shower before dinner."

"Of course, go ahead... I'll clean up and take one also, but first I have to put away these toys and hide my bag so you don't ruin my future surprises." He laughs.

Sarah nods and walks away in the direction of his guest bathroom. He watches her pretty ass wiggle from side to side with every step. He smiles to himself as it's totally marked up with bright red stripes from the strap, and reddish purple hand prints from the spanking he just gave her. He hears the shower running and quickly grabs his phone. He sends a short text to Mrs. Doyle that reads.

"Mission accomplished over here. She's taking a shower so I don't have long. Did you check out the videos and website I sent?

Mrs. Doyle texted her response back to him.

"I sure did and I loved them! Thank you so much for sending them! I had to take of myself once already and I plan on watching many more tonight. I'll need to put new batteries in my vibrator." She ends it with a smiley face emoji.

"LOL, Glad that you're enjoying them. It's all because of you that I found them and this side of me has awakened. So, once again, I have to say THANK YOU. The shower just stopped so she'll be coming out. Delete these texts and don't send another. I'll talk to you tomorrow."

Caleb ends his text and actually turns his phone completely off.

He then heads into his bedroom, locks his bathroom door to prevent Sarah from popping in and takes his shower. He returns shortly after to his kitchen, completely clean and fresh. Sarah is there having just finished setting the table and has heated up their dinner. He doesn't waste a minute and quickly embraces her with a tender hug and a super sexy kiss.

"Mmm… Yummy!… That might be even better than dinner." She says with her sexy giggle.

They proceeded to sit down and Caleb was ready to answer all her questions. There was no way in hell that he was going to tell her about his neighbor, Mrs. Doyle and how she was the catalyst for all this new found kink. Plus, there's absolutely no chance that he's going to tell her about the spanking that she just gave him and their agreement for future discipline. He's honoring his promise to keep that secret just between him and Mrs. Doyle.

Caleb definitely needed some extra time to formulate a story and come up with believable lies for his kinky behavior. The shower he just took gave him just that. He turns to Sarah and is ready to address all of her questions.

"So where would you like me to start, babe?" He asked.

She drops her head down and gives him a look, "Um… Let's see… BDSM? Spanking? Toys?" She replies with a little of her own sarcasm.

Caleb comes up with quite a story to cover his ass… literally!

"Last year, on my 21rst birthday, my friends surprised me and hired a Dominatrix. I had no idea and I thought they were just taking me to a strip club. They blindfolded me and drove me to this location and walked me into her place. Then they left and said "See you in an hour, buddy.""

"Wow! OMG!" Sarah laughs, "That's something my girlfriends would do to me."

She totally falls for Caleb's whale of a story. He continues to elaborate and embellish the details even more.

"So, while I was still blindfolded, I felt my arms getting tied up with rope, just like I did to you. Then the blindfold was removed and this very attractive, slightly older woman was standing there in front of me. She had a stern look on her face and was holding a leather strap. She told me that I have been a very bad boy and that she was going to give me a serious spanking."

"Holy shit! No way!" Sarah responds with a giggle.

Caleb laughs along with her, "And boy did she!… She stripped me down to my birthday suit and went to town on my ass with that leather strap. She put me in several different positions and also spanked me with a wooden spoon, and a riding crop. That's where I learned about safe words, rope, spanking, etc." Caleb adds, "I learned so much from her… and of course I learned a lot watching BDSM, spanking, and porn videos."

"Did you have sex with her?" Sarah asks with wide eyed curiosity.

"No, not at all... She never took her clothes off. However, after she thoroughly reddened my ass, she fingered me, used a butt plug on me, and stroked me until I came." Caleb continues with his whale of a fabricated story.

"So, it's obvious that you're really into spanking... Why didn't you tell me?" Sarah questions him.

"We've only been together for a little over a month, babe. I wanted to make sure our relationship was strong enough for me to share my kinky secrets with you. Plus, I didn't know that you would be into it." He replies, "Not everyone is into getting spanked or being kinky." Caleb is actually impressed with his own story and his answers to her questions.

"Well, that was the first time I've ever been spanked." Sarah replies, "I absolutely loved it!... Let me clarify... I found it to be sexy and I was so turned on by everything that you did to me. I loved how you combined pleasure, then pain, then back to pleasure. Plus, having me blindfolded and tied up with no control. That was so freaking hot!"

Caleb smiles and replies, "I know I spanked you really hard at the end and you had to use your safe word."

"Haha... Yeah, my ass is marked up and still on fire right now, but I really loved it." She laughs, "I guess I won't be wearing my bathing suit or my skimpy little shorts for a while."

Sarah continued to ask him more questions. "So did you spank your past girlfriends? Did they spank you?"

"No, not really. Just a few slaps on the ass during sex. I was saving showing off my kinky side and my toys for the right girl and the right time." Caleb replies and chuckles, "... and here you are!"

"Well, I'm not sure how I got so lucky... You know that I've only had two sex partners before you." She reiterates and continues, "So, all this kinky stuff is totally new to me, but I'm completely open and willing to try more."

Caleb smiles at her and before he can say anything in return, Sarah continues to ramble on.

"Hell babe, I would love to try spanking you." She smirks, "Or even better yet, I would love to see a Dominatrix spank you. It would be so hot watching another woman handle you, plus imagine what I could learn from her."

Sarah once again concludes with her cute, sexy laugh that instantly makes him smile.

"What if I want to see the Dominatrix spank you?" Caleb asks her, "I would love to watch an attractive, mature woman redden your ass and put you in your place."

"Oooh, bring it on..." She giggles once again. "Hey, we could have her spank us both!"

"Damn, this conversation just keeps getting better and better!" He replies with a sexy smirk on his face.

Chapter 21

Caleb laughs along with Sarah and is beyond surprised at her response. He never thought that she would be so open and willing to dive into these kinky adventures. Especially since they've only been together for a short time.

He knows it's rare to have this type of trust along with a try-anything-attitude in a relationship that's so new. It's definitely something that he's never experienced before, since just about every one of his past girlfriends had been super possessive. He's kind of feeling guilty for telling her such a huge lie and completely fabricated story. Had he known that her reaction would've been this nonchalant, he might have just told her the truth about getting a spanking from Mrs. Doyle. Of course, it would have betrayed his neighbors trust to share their secret, but maybe this wouldn't of been a bad thing. His mind is now getting filled with images of his mature and attractive neighbor spanking both him and Sarah together. He's momentarily lost in this daydream and has a slightly perplexed look on his face. This makes Sarah think that she said something wrong and she quickly wants to clarify her response.

"I may be inexperienced, but I'm definitely not a prude, babe." Sarah tells him, "You might be shocked at what I find sexy."

Caleb quickly jumps in and is dying to hear her inner thoughts, "Well tell me… I just opened up and shared everything about my kinky nature with you."

Sarah pauses for a moment and gathers her thoughts before replying to him.

"I find being watched sexy. I guess that's why I was so turned on when you blindfolded and tied me up. Some of that was knowing that I was on display sort of speak… to you." She replies.

"Ah, you like being an exhibitionist," Caleb responds.

"Not totally... I mean... I wouldn't want to do it somewhere that would really put me in danger. However, I've seen some movies where people are watching others and I love the thought of being watched and being desired. That's a huge turn-on for me." She divulges.

"Really? So are you saying that you want to be a stripper?" Caleb asks.

"No, not at all. Although, I do like the idea of burlesque. I recently went to see a couple girls on the softball team that are in this burlesque troupe. They perform weekly all around the state. It was a really, really good show. It was sexy but yet classy and the costumes, props, and their dancing skills were amazing!" She clarifies, "It's cabaret with the right amount of risk and sexiness."

"So you should look into joining their troupe." Caleb quickly replies.

"Yeah, I might. It could be really fun and a great side income. Olivia, one of the girls, constantly asks me to join them. However, I don't want anything to get in the way of my softball and my studies. Plus, that's not really the type of exhibitionism that really turns me on." Sarah answers.

Caleb, not fully understanding, instantly replies, "Well, what is the type that turns you on?"

"I have a few... I've seen a couple of movies where people are at a masquerade type party or private club and they have hot sex with others watching... That would be a huge turn on for me. I also wouldn't mind being the one watching as other attractive people fuck each others brains out." She laughs.

"Whoa, that is hot!" Caleb replies, "I wouldn't mind trying either of those as long as it's a safe environment."

"Yep, I agree." Sarah chimes in and asks, "So you wouldn't mind being watched?"

Caleb takes a moment to think about it and replies.

"Hmmm... I'm not sure if I would like to be the one on display in front of a large group of people. However, if I was on display in front of just a few girls or women, I would find that extremely hot." He then elaborates, "One thing for sure is, I know that I would like to watch others. After all, I already admitted to you that I like to watch kinky porn and spanking videos. So, it would be a huge turn on to see stuff like that in person, especially a spanking."

Caleb doesn't let on that he already knows all about seeing a spanking firsthand. After all, that's what got him totally infatuated with his neighbor, Mrs. Doyle. He also knows that he would love to be on display, at least in front of a few women. He has an instant flashback of everything that his friend Ryder shared on that day when he was fully exposed and spanked by his mom and Mrs. Beck.

Caleb had already pictured himself and fantasized about being in that exact scenario that Ryder was in. His perverted mind has created an entire movie where Mrs. Doyle and Mrs. Beck aggressively strip him bare and administer a serious disciplining. He pictures the stern women intently staring at every inch of his body as he dances in pain from the effects of their leather strap.

Of course, he continues to play it cool and doesn't give Sarah any suspicions that he's already masturbated several times to the scenario of being watched, handled, and disciplined by multiple women at the same time.

"Well, since I now know that I like to be spanked, I would find it hot to watch someone getting spanked as well." She smirks and then adds, "Maybe we can go to a spanking club or event together?"

"That would be incredibly hot!" Caleb replies, "I'll search the internet to see what's out there."

Caleb is beyond happy to know that his girlfriend has this sexy and kinky side within her that she's willing to explore. She must actually be clairvoyant because she continues to totally surprise Caleb with her responses.

"Stick with me, Caleb… For your next birthday, I might have to hire 1 or even 2 attractive, older women to spank you in front of me and a few of my cute girlfriends. I'm sure they would love to see that body of yours totally naked and watch it all happen!" She tells him with a sexy smirk.

Caleb is completely floored and tries to shrug it off with humor, "Oh, C'mon babe… Don't make me wait that long. I just had a birthday."

"Oh, don't worry… I don't want to wait that long either to see that!" Sarah replies in a tone that is completely serious, "Just be careful what you wish for, honey!"

Caleb knows it's a fact that seeing the way Mrs. Doyle gave Dillon that bare bottom spanking on Friday night, was the catalyst for all this. It was the incentive and reason for him to visit spanking websites, watch videos, and create a couple of profiles on BDSM and fetish websites.

Now add to that, his conversation with Mrs. Doyle this afternoon, in which he came right out and asked her to discipline him. That resulted in them both getting incredibly turned on, especially Mrs. Doyle. The moment she stripped him of his clothing and took in the sight of his amazing physique, she was a goner. She couldn't help but love every minute of forcefully handling him and spanking his bare ass with her thick leather strap. Not only does Caleb have the looks of a super model, he has an ass that is as delightfully round as it is toned and muscular.

Caleb was more than turned on himself, having his stunningly attractive neighbor, who is twice his age, handle him with such force. He not only thought of her in a romantic way, but even more so, he fantasized about her as a strict disciplinarian. That fantasy turned to reality for him a few short hours ago. This didn't just turn him on, it super-charged every fiber in his young, athletic body.

Caleb was sprouting an erection so big that it could rival a baseball bat.

They both shared a bunch of secrets with each other, and have now formed this kinky relationship. Caleb is chomping at the bit to get more spankings from her. He's also planning his own revenge and fantasizing about getting at her sexy body. Those wide hips, and that plump ass of hers drive him wild every time he sees her. Not only does he want to spank her, he also wants to fuck her into the hemisphere… every which way possible! He already knew from her own admittance, that she'd been stifling that sexy, kinky side of hers for the past 20 years. Jim Doyle, her husband, is a cool guy and an awesome neighbor, but according to her, he's as vanilla as a bowl of ice cream. Simply put, Megan Doyle, wants, needs, and craves so much more… And Caleb, her young neighbor, is just the guy to give it to her!

These events alone would be enough to send anyone over the moon, but for a 22-year-old hormone-raging guy… it's epic! Now his girlfriend, Sarah, has just got a taste of this world and is begging for more! It's crazy to think that all of this happened in literally 24 hours.

Who knows what else will happen come tomorrow?

After all, Mr. Doyle and his sons are still away camping, which leaves Mrs. Doyle home alone. Caleb's young mind is running a mile a minute with thoughts ranging from romantic to incredibly kinky.

There's one thing that's for certain. From this moment on, spanking and discipline are going to be a huge part of Caleb's life. Actually, it might prove to be a bigger part of his girlfriend Sarah's and his neighbor, Mrs. Megan Doyle's life as well.

Caleb stops to think of both of these super hot, super amazing women in his life. The ultimate would be to have them both… at the same time!

Meanwhile, Megan Doyle is next-door pleasuring herself again as she fantasizes about Caleb. Her mind is uncovering everything that's been buried deep inside her, and it's just exploding with an abundance of fresh, kinky ideas.

She quivers uncontrollably and climaxes for the second time in an hour. She revels in the feeling as her body slowly stops shaking and she comes back down from cloud nine. She knows Pandora's Box has now been opened, and she's more than ready to release everything she had stored in it.

Her fingers take one last plunge into her own vagina as she coats them with her own juices. She then places her fingers in her mouth to taste herself. She smirks as she confidently knows this kinky, sexy side of her has know been reawakened.

For all of them...This is the weekend that started it all... The Weekend That Changed Everything!

Chapter 22

The early morning sun begins to peak through Caleb's bedroom window, signaling the start of a bright, beautiful day ahead. His girlfriend Sarah wakes up and quietly heads down the hall straight for the shower in the guest bathroom. She's extremely considerate, since only her and the birds are awake, as Caleb remains in bed fast asleep. After the warmth of a hot shower rains down on her, she wraps her body in an over-sized bath towel and proceeds with a simple, quick morning routine of brushing her teeth, applying deodorant, and towel-drying her hair. She's pressed for time and due at the college campus for an early morning baseball practice, and team vaccinations.

The stunning 20-year-old athletic beauty drops the towel and takes a moment and gives a good look at herself in the full-length bathroom mirror. Sometimes it doesn't matter if you're old or young, totally in shape or not, women have a way of picking themselves apart and letting their deepest insecurities come out. Everything from my boobs are too small to these dimples on my ass and my cellulite looks awful, goes through our minds constantly.

However, today for some reason, Sarah is feeling very confident as she stares at herself in her birthday suit. Of course, anyone that has seen her naked would think she's heaven on earth. With her somewhat curly, long, brown hair, complimented by her big brown eyes, and olive skin, her beauty is as natural as can be. Those who've had the privilege of seeing her body naked, including, the girls on her baseball team, would all agree that she is a total stunner. It's just about a daily occurrence in the locker room after practice that she feels several of her teammates hands gently slapping her cute, round, bubble butt as they disguise it with "Great job out there!".

Most of these soft pats come from Coach Miranda, a strong and absolutely beautiful, mature woman who is twice her age. The hard-ass coach isn't typically known for giving her players compliments. However, she always manages to make an exception with Sarah. There's no doubt that Sarah has a rear-end that just calls for attention, but also because she is the star of her college baseball team. Sarah alone might just be the main factor in the success of her team and the reason why they've won two back-to-back championships.

She takes one last look at herself in the mirror, letting her eyes scan her entire body. Her fitness routine is on point as she flexes her abs, as well as her arms, and approves of the muscle tone she sees. She then turns to take in a view of her own booty, and manages to display a smile so bright that it rivals the morning sun. Her smile is mostly due to viewing the thick, red marks that are displayed across both of her ass cheeks.

Caleb's dominance and the way he handled her last night, by spanking her, using blindfolds, restraints, and toys, awakened something deep inside her soul. It was life-changing and she loved every single part of it and she knew, from now on, that would be a huge part of her sexuality. Sarah definitely isn't used to being controlled, as several of her past boyfriends will attest to. She's way too focused and goal-oriented, which mistakenly gives her a reputation of being bitchy instead of driven. On the surface level, Sarah could easily be the one to administer the discipline. She just has that type of vibe. She would even admit that she's much more the bossy type, and very similar to the personality of Coach Miranda.

She admires the warmth and compassion combined with the strength and no-nonsense approach of her college baseball coach that has already led her school to win multiple championships. Coach Miranda is not only beautiful on the inside, but she's an absolutely stunning woman with a figure that stops traffic. Sarah often compares herself to Miranda, who is more than twice her age and even finds herself constantly looking over to steal a glimpse of her coach's toned arms and curvy figure. But what really gets Sarah's attention, is Coach Miranda's perfectly round, ample bottom.

Even though Caleb totally blew her mind last night, Sarah's been harvesting a huge secret herself. She can't deny the attraction that she has to her coach. It's safe to say that the majority of times that she's pleasured herself with her vibrator, it wasn't because she was thinking of Caleb, it was because her mind was lost in various sexual fantasies involving Coach Miranda.

Sarah realizes that she's equally drawn to both guys and girls. However, so far, she's kept that under wraps and has never experienced being with another girl. The truth is, as beautiful and stunning as she is, she's only had a handful of boyfriends. Most guys don't even try to approach her in fear that she's way out of their league.

There's something about Sarah that just exudes confidence to all that meet her and yet, she still has her own moments of insecurity. She still plenty of doubts as she tries to understand and connect her mind to her body. Last night with Caleb might just be the sexual-awakening and coming of age experience that she so desperately needed… in more ways than one!

With all that on her mind, she takes one last look at her red-marked bottom in the bathroom mirror. She smiles to herself in approval as she tiptoes back into the bedroom and maneuvers herself quietly over to the side of the bed. She's being extra careful not to wake him up just yet as she has plans to really make him rise. Her totally naked body is glistening in the glow of the faint morning sunlight that's attempting to peak through the blinds of his bedroom window.

She gently pulls the covers off him and takes in the sight of him sleeping in his pajama bottoms without a shirt. The fact that he's not totally naked is actually more tempting to her. She places her mouth on his pajamas over his penis and starts kissing, licking, and rubbing him.

She then reaches her hand into the cutout in the front of his pajamas and gently guides his dick into her mouth. She engulfs every inch of it right down to his testicles, and proceeds to vigorously go to town licking and sucking him. Caleb is somewhat startled as he comes out of his deep sleep. Still, in a groggy state, he feels the magic of her tongue all over the shaft of his penis, and reaches his hands out to touch her.

"Mmm, good morning, baby." He murmurs as his dick becomes completely erect.

Sarah intercepts his hands and quickly pins his arms away.

"Keep those hands away and just lay there, mister!" She tells him in a stern voice, "I gotta get to practice, but I wanted to give you a little something before I left."

Caleb feels her hands lower his pajama bottoms as he lays flat on his back, watching her blow him to ecstasy. Sarah might not have a lot of sexual experience, but what she does have is an incredibly sexy mind and that drive to be the best at everything she does. Right now with Caleb, she has a desire to please and wants him to start his day remembering her and getting the blowjob of his life. Her beautiful plush lips and that amazing tongue of hers feels like heaven all over his dick. Caleb's breathing begins to get heavy as her hand starts stroking him in unison with her sucking.

"Ahh... Yes!" Caleb reacts and she knows that he's moments away from orgasm.

She flicks her tongue across the head of his penis as her hand strokes him at a feverish pace. Caleb's body starts to shake as he erupts like a volcano and moans with pleasure.

"Mmmm... Oh!"

Sarah places her entire mouth over his penis and catches every drop of his sperm. It's the first time she's ever swallowed, and once again, Caleb is caught by surprise from her actions. She makes sure he's totally finished before taking her mouth away and fetching a towel for him. She returns with a smile on her face that's a perfect match to the one that he has painted across his face.

"That was one hell of a surprise, baby!... What a way to wake me up... You are so fucking sexy!" He complimented her.

"I needed to return the favor for everything you did to me last night." She replies, "My ass is so sore, but I love it!"

She turns around and shows him that luscious ass of hers that's completely bruised and marked with his hand prints along with stripes from the leather strap. Caleb takes in the view and just smirks.

"So I guess you slept on your stomach, huh babe?" Caleb laughs.

"Haha very funny, baby… You just wait until I get my hands on your ass… But, truthfully, I was up for at least another two, maybe even three hours, after you fell asleep." She tells him, "I watched a ton of spanking videos and some BDSM porn also. It got me heated up all over again. I was worried that I was going to wake you up, so I slipped into the bathroom and played with myself until I came."

Her confession makes Caleb smile so brightly that it lights up the entire room.

"No way!" He responds, "You little freak!"

Sarah couldn't help but laugh, "Hey, a girl has to do what a girl has to do!"

"So tell me about some of the videos that really turned you on. I hope you bookmarked them. I need to check them out. Do you have a favorite?"

"Oh God, I have several favorites." She replies, "I watched a ton of Dominatrix videos. I love the idea of tying someone up, taking their control away, and doing all kinds of kinky things to them. Basically, the way you handled me last night and more… I hope you're ready because I can't wait to dominate you and try some of those things I've seen on video!"

Caleb loves hearing his girlfriend talk sexy like this. For her it just comes naturally. After all, she is a Scorpio and she just exudes sexiness. It's not only in the way she talks, but it's also in the things that she doesn't say. It's in the way she carries herself and will just shoot him over a certain look. It's also her complete openness to dive in and try new things, often without even hesitating.

"What else?" He asks her.

"Of course, I love the videos where someone is getting a serious spanking. Not just little love taps, but a real serious spanking… squirming and struggling with tears and marks… That really turns me on!" She replies and continues to elaborate.

"I watched some really hot videos with people role-playing. I love the scenarios such as school principal/student, police officer/lawbreaker, boss/employee, and doctor/patient. Those totally got me going! Especially, the ones that have multiple people giving a spanking or getting spanked… But, more importantly, I learned about the various spanking positions like Over The Knee, Over The Hip, Diaper Position, and Wheelbarrow. I also watched how to limit squirming and wiggling by interlocking a single leg or even both legs. You also can hold their arm behind their back so they can't block your spanks. I learned so much from watching spanking porn last night. It's freaking crazy!"

Sarah's excitement about spanking couldn't be contained. Caleb can't believe his ears and how quickly his girlfriend had gained all this knowledge and interest in spanking. He quickly confirms that he's totally onboard.

"Wow! I'm impressed…" He comments back, "That's how I got many of the ideas to dominate you."

He continues to tell her, "In addition to having that dominatrix experience that my friends got me for my 21st birthday, I also watched a bunch of videos that had spanking scenes. Now I'm totally hooked! The next thing I knew was I'm reading more stories, looking for spanking pictures, and buying leather straps, riding crops, handcuffs, blindfolds… Fucking crazy! It was never even on my radar before, and now I can't stop thinking about it. I'm just thankful that you're into it. Imagine the fun we are going to have together."

"Oh, it's going to be fun, alright." Sarah sarcastically responds as she sends him a strong, sexy look.

"Just wait until I tie you up and spank your ass!" She tells him with that stern look in her big brown eyes.

"I'm about to get another hard-on if you keep talking like that." He replies back.

"Well, you're lucky that I have to get to practice. However, you can bet that getting my revenge and giving you a spanking will be on my mind." She tells him, "I'm even going to start getting my own supplies!"

"Oh My God!... You would make the most amazing Domme ever!" Caleb smirks, "You have that personality and that fire inside of you. Plus, you would absolutely rock any outfit that you put on!"

Sarah quickly chimes in, "I can totally see myself doing that. Plus, it might just be financially rewarding also. I'll have to look into that once I turn 21 next month. How would you feel about that? I mean… Would you be okay with the spanking people for money?"

"Hmmm, I guess..." Caleb pauses to think about it more and then continues, "As long as I didn't include full-on sex. It would be like attending a spanking event, but you would actually be getting paid for it. Hell, I might look into that also! It's much more interesting than programming computers." He ends with a laugh.

Sarah definitely didn't expect that response at all from him. Especially, since this relationship is so new. In the past, her boyfriends were always the smothering type, and this new freedom with Caleb is a breath of fresh air.

Caleb looks intently at her, "I don't own you Sarah. Trust is something that we both need to have if this relationship is going to work. We just need to establish some clear guidelines."

Sarah jumps in and adds, "When you told me about your Dominatrix experience, you mentioned that she didn't take any of her clothes off... right?"

"Nope! She didn't... As I mentioned, she used implements and toys on me, stroked me, and fingered me until I came. For her it was all business and part of her job. Even though I'm not super thrilled at the thought of you doing those things to other guys, I can't be a hypocrite."

Sarah was actually surprised to hear Caleb's openness about this subject. Even though it was just a passing thought she had to be a professional Dominatrix, she's actually really impressed with his mindset. She even gets a tingle through her body as she pictures herself in this way.

"You know, I would still want to be spanked as well at times. So I guess that makes me a switch." She tells him.

"Well, I'm here for you, babe." Caleb quickly added with laughter, "You already know, I'll redden your ass anytime!"

Sarah asks, "Caleb, what if I wanted to get spanked by an older, mature woman?... That would be something I would really like to experience."

He laughs and concludes, "I'm cool with you getting spanked by a woman. Hell, invite me along to watch."

"Ha! Figures... Typical guy response." Sarah replies with sarcasm. "We can talk more later. I gotta get to practice and then get vaccinated. Everyone on the team has to be vaccinated if we want to play this year. Thankfully, the vaccinations go in the arm and they won't see my ass."

"Haha…" Caleb laughed. "Yeah, that's right. You need to remember that your ass is really marked up. So be careful when you're in the locker room, showering, and getting changed, unless you want all your teammates to know." He chuckles again as he reminds her.

"Oh shit! Thanks for reminding me. I'll make sure I shower at home after practice." She replies.

Sarah finishes getting dressed as Caleb lays in bed and revels in the moment. She then grabs her gym bag and prepares to head to school for the team's 9am meeting. Before she walks out his bedroom door, she tells him one additional thing.

"Hey babe, check your text messages. I've attached a video that I think you'll really like. It's for your eyes only. You'll see exactly what I was doing last night while you were sleeping!" She tells him in a sexy tone.

"Can't wait!" Caleb replied.

"I feel things changing sexually with me. I feel more open and adventurous and it's all because of you. Who knows?" Sarah smirks at him, "this could be the weekend that changes everything for me."

Her sexy banter makes him smile from ear to ear as he watches her leave his bedroom. He rolls over and drifts back to get a few more hours of sleep as Sarah exits his house and is on route for her 9am practice.

About fifteen minutes later, Sarah arrives at the baseball field and greets her teammates. They are already standing in front of the field house as instructed. Sarah, and her best friend Olivia, are giggling and talking up a storm. Coach Miranda is off a short distance away to the left, in front of a large white tent that's been set up. She's talking with a nurse and a few assistants who are organizing paperwork. All conversations all come to an end as Coach Miranda walks over and addresses the team.

"Okay girls... Have your medical forms, proof of vaccines, and blood work results ready. Those that aren't vaccinated form one line right here." She points to a spot next to where she's standing right outside the large tent.

The team quickly divides itself with the majority of girls standing in the unvaccinated line. Sarah and Olivia are part of this majority as they reach for the paperwork from their recent physical exams. Coach Miranda waits to see the lines form and gives more instructions.

"For those of you vaccinated, hand in your forms and proceed to the weight room and do your workout." Coach instructs and continues, "For those in this line needing the vaccine, fill out this form."

Two of the assistants hand out forms attached to clipboards and pens to the girls in this line. Coach Miranda introduces Nurse Natalie along with her assistants and delivers a bit of news regarding the vaccine to the girls.

"Hey Team, this is Nurse Natalie and these are her assistants Chloe and Michaela." She continues, "Here's how it's going to work. Michaela, will be collecting your forms and then one at a time I'll call your name to enter the tent. Since we have a game in a couple of days, the vaccines will not be given in your right or left arm as usual. We are not risking anyone having a sore arm that can affect your playing, throwing, or batting. Therefore, all vaccines today will be given to you in your rear end."

These words are followed up by a few mumbles as the girls react to Coach Miranda's news.

Chapter 23

Some of the girls turn to look at each other as they really don't have an option if they want to play for the team this year. Sarah remains silent but her face turns beet red with embarrassment. She normally wouldn't have a problem and she's more than used to being naked, showering, and changing in the locker room with the team. However, this morning she knows the marks on her ass will absolutely draw attention to anyone that sees them.

"So, once you are inside the tent," Coach Miranda continues, "Go straight to the table… Pants and panties come down, make sure your booty is completely exposed, and bend over the table for your shot. Is that clear?"

Coach Miranda concludes as a wave of silence comes over her players. None of the players ask any questions as they remain in line filling out their forms. Once all the forms are handed in, Coach Miranda puts them in the order of the girls in line and begins to call the names one by one.

"Emma, step into the tent." Coach Miranda calls out, then steps back into the tent with Emma.

The cute student follows orders and walks over to the table. She lowers her leggings together with her panties and bends over the table. Assistant Michaela prepares the syringe and sets it out on a tray table for Nurse Natalie. Assistant Chloe opens an alcohol wipe and rubs it on the area of Emma's right butt cheek where the injection will be given. She then steps away as Nurse Natalie approaches with the needle.

"Okay, Emma… A little pinch." Nurse Natalie announces as her fingers grab a small area of Emma's butt cheek. She then presses the needle into Emma's rear end.

"Ooo!" Emma reacts and makes a small sound from the injection.

"All done." Nurse Natalie replies as she disposes of the syringe and signs her name on the paperwork.

Chloe presses another clean swab over the area of Emma's butt to prevent bleeding. She then applies a Band-Aid as Michaela hands Emma her the signed medical form and proof of her vaccine. Coach Miranda looks on as Emma pulls her clothing back up and walks out of the tent.

This routine continues and at least 4 more girls get their vaccinations. Just then, Coach Miranda steps out of the tent and calls out, "Sarah… you're next... come on in."

So far, everything had been running like clockwork and Coach Miranda is more than impressed with the organization of Nurse Natalie and her assistants. She's a huge fan of team work and structure where everyone has a function and works together to get the job done. This is exactly what she's witnessing from Nurse Natalie and her assistants, Chloe and Michaela, as she oversees her players enter the tent and get their mandatory vaccines.

Sarah, still showing signs of embarrassment all over her face, enters the tent and approaches the exam table. She keeps her head straight forward and avoids making eye contact with Coach Miranda, Nurse Natalie, and her assistants. She lowers her clothing and exposes her bare, marked up, bottom as she positions herself bent over the table.

Chloe is the first to notice as she remains quiet and does her job of rubbing the alcohol wipe onto Sarah's bruised cheeks. Once she's done, she signals to Nurse Natalie, who now approaches with the needle. Nurse Natalie takes in the full view of Sarah's bottom and makes a sound to clear her throat, which causes Coach Miranda to turn her head and look.

"Well honey, I'm not sure what you did to get that spanking, but I'm afraid this will hurt a bit more than usual." Nurse Natalie tells her.

Sarah remains silent and doesn't say a word as now everyone in the tent, including Coach Miranda and assistant Michaela, take in the full view of her bare bottom. Sarah, is of course, embarrassed but also a bit turned on, as this feeds into the exhibitionist side of her. She turns her head to the side as she hears Coach Miranda walking closer to the table where she's bent over. She now makes eye contact with her coach, who has a look of concern on her face. She looks over and notices everyone under the tent are completely focusing their eyes on her bare red-marked bottom. She then feels Coach Miranda trace her fingers over the red strap marks on her cheeks.

"Sarah, I would like to have a word with you after your vaccine." Coach Miranda tells her.

Sarah just nods her head in a yes motion as she feels Nurse Natalie press the needle into her rear end. She grits her teeth and refrains from making a sound.

"Okay, all done," Nurse Natalie announces as once again Chloe follows up with her tasks.

"Sarah, come with me. Let's go to the office in the field house." Coach tells her as she hands the forms to Michaela to take over.

Sarah pulls her clothing back up and follows her coach out of the tent. Assistant Michaela steps out right behind them and calls out.

"Olivia, you're next... come on in."

Olivia walks toward the tent and passes her friend and the coach leaving together. She knows something isn't right based on the look Sarah has displayed on her face. She also notices the look of concern on Coach Miranda's face and reacts.

"Sarah, you okay?" Olivia calls out to her.

Before Sarah can even answer, Coach Miranda responds, "She might be dehydrated so I'm going to sit with her for a bit and give her some Gatorade."

"Sarah, text me if you need anything. I'll check in with you after my workout." Olivia tells her.

"Thanks Liv, I will." Sarah replied.

As Olivia heads into the tent to receive her vaccine, Sarah and Coach Miranda enter the field house and retreat to an office. Coach Miranda closes the door as they take a seat. She still has that look of concern all over her face as she begins to speak.

"Sarah, first of all, I want you know, that this is a safe place. I'm a safe place… You can confide in me and I will assure your safety. As a staff member, we are trained to be on the lookout for abuse, domestic violence, drug usage, and many other things. So, after seeing those marks all over your backside, I needed to check on you." Coach expresses with a sincere tone and then continues.

"Are you being abused?"
"You can tell me everything in complete confidence." She concludes and waits for Sarah's response.

Sarah gives an embarrassed smirk that turns into a slight smile as she responds.

"Oh, God no!" She replies, "It's not like that all coach… I'm a little embarrassed to tell you, but the truth is that my boyfriend dominated me last night. He totally surprised me. I was always safe and I could've stopped him at anytime. I'm so sorry that I alarmed you but there is absolutely no cause for concern."

"Oh God, I'm so sorry, Sarah… I didn't even think about that." Coach Miranda replies, "I know that you're a straight A student and I immediately thought the worse… Please accept my apology."

Sarah chuckles, "It's Okay Coach… and thank you for looking out for me… for all of us. That says a lot about how amazing you are!"

Sarah actually stands up and gives Coach Miranda a huge, warm hug. Her words and their embrace quickly changed Coach Miranda's face from displaying that concerned look to a bright, somewhat curious smile.

"Well, your secret is safe with me and I'll make sure Nurse Natalie and her assistants honor your privacy as well." Coach responds.

"Thanks Coach. I will be extremely careful when changing and I also plan on showering at home so that no one on the team sees these marks." Sarah grins and chuckles.

Coach Miranda replies, "Haha… based on that smile on your face, they might want to experience exactly what you got. You better guard your boyfriend… He might become a hot commodity with a high demand!" She laughs and jokes, "Hell, I might even pursue him. Lord knows that I can use a little kink in my life. It sounds like fun and exactly what I need!"

Sarah flat out laughs at Coach Miranda's response about her boyfriend and needing some kink in her life. She makes sure that her coach knows that this won't affect her playing or practicing.

"Coach, I can assure you that this doesn't impact my playing or practicing in any way. It looks worse than it really is. My butt is only a little tender when I sit or press on it." Sarah comments with a slight laugh.

Coach Miranda pauses for a moment to think about it and then responds, "I'll tell you what… Take today off from practice and working out. I'll tell the team that you were dehydrated and needed to rest. This way, no one will suspect anything."

"That's not necessary, Coach. I want to practice and work out." Sarah replies.

"Sarah, I insist about taking today off from practice. As for working out, maybe you can just wait and do your workout later today when everyone from the team has gone home." Coach comments.

"No problem, coach. As for getting a little kink in your life... I highly recommend it." Sarah smirks and continues, "I saw the way the new assistant football coach was looking at you. He's totally hot and that strong, muscular body of his is really sexy. I bet he would give you a good spanking."

Sarah's words make her coach laugh out loud as they continue to form an even closer bond over this bizarre conversation.

Coach Miranda replies with a chuckle, "Yeah, I bet he would give a good spanking, but don't assume anything... I might be the one that wants to dominate and give the spanking!"

Sarah's flirty nature comes through loud and clear as she wastes no time in responding, "Well, in that case I volunteer. I loved getting my ass spanked. Even though it hurt like hell, it turned me on more than I would've ever imagined."

"Is that so?" Coach Miranda asks her with a sarcastic, playful tone.

"Yep, for sure!" Sarah replies, "I can't wait to explore more spanking and even BDSM. I'm totally hooked and uninhibited. I want to experience anything and everything about it... giving...getting... I especially want to watch someone get a good spanking and have others watch me getting spanked."

Coach Miranda first displays a complex look on her face that quickly turns into an expression that shows she understands what Sarah is telling her. She nods her head in a "Yes" motion and replies.

"You know... I get it... I need to revisit this area of my life with no inhibitions." Coach realizes and elaborates, "I've always been a very controlling person but at times I do crave giving up control and having someone else take charge. That's always been a void in my life."

Sarah's young mind instantly processes what Miranda said. She reflects on the conversation she just had with Caleb about pursuing her dominant side. With no hesitation, she replied back to her coach.

"I can help with that void. Let me show you the way my boyfriend handled me… The exact positions he used, the implements...everything! I had no control and no inhibitions last night, yet I was totally safe. I highly recommend it… It was the best feeling ever!"

"Hmmm. Are you sure about that young lady?" Coach Miranda responds as she remains close in Sarah's personal space after their hug, "Cause if you are, count me in… I would absolutely love that!"

Chapter 24

Sarah feels the attraction to her coach and stares intently into her eyes. She feels her vagina pulse as it gets a little moist after hearing Coach Miranda's response. Before she can even muster another response, Coach Miranda's hand touches her face and their lips connect into a sexy kiss.

Sarah opens her mouth to receive Coach Miranda's tongue as she experiences her first kiss by a woman. This isn't like the kiss her friend Olivia told her that she received from a girl at a party during a truth or dare game. Instead, this is a very sexy and passionate kiss from an older, very attractive woman who is also an authority figure in her life.

The chemistry is electrifying as they both embrace each other tighter while their tongues collide. Sarah couldn't help but notice the difference in the way Coach Miranda's plush lips feel against hers. Even though she loves the way Caleb's lips feel, this kiss feels totally different and just as good, if not better, than his.

She lets her hands wander down to feel Coach Miranda's curvy hips and then places them over her ass. She gives a little squeeze through the fabric of her coach's thin, dark gray yoga tights. Coach Miranda feels Sarah's hands grab her butt and she lets out a soft, little moan as her breathing intensifies, "Mmm!"

Sarah feels the wetness in her vagina increase as she hears her coach moan with delight. She opens her mouth even wider and makes sure that her tongue explores every inch of Coach Miranda's mouth. Coach Miranda sinks even more into this kiss as her hands wander down and touch Sarah's amazing body. She ends the kiss with a soft little bite on Sarah's plush red lips. Sarah responds with a smile to the sexy little bite and grabs Miranda's ass a little harder.

"Oooh… grabbing my ass huh?" Coach Miranda comments, emphasizing certain words, "You ARE a bad girl!... I may need to give YOU a good spanking!"

Sarah quickly flirts back, "I'm a really naughty girl... I think you should definitely spank me!"

Coach Miranda reaches down and grabs a handful of Sarah's ass over her thin, black leggings. Sarah responds with a little wince from the force of Coach Miranda's grip on her tender rear end. Coach Miranda is so caught up in the moment that she totally forgot about the state of her student's sore bottom. She notices the facial expression and reaction that Sarah makes.

"Oh my God, I'm so sorry. I totally forgot that you are sore back there." Coach apologizes.

Sara replies with her cute laugh, "It's okay... I like pain... remember?"

Coach Miranda smiles as her hands gently pat Sarah's bottom. She places her mouth over Sarah's left ear and whispers.

"Oh, I can't wait to spank that beautiful ass of yours. However, let's wait until it's healed. This way I'll be able to see my hand prints on it."

Sarah's juices trickled down her legs after hearing that sexy whisper in her ear. It would be a total fantasy for her to experience a spanking from Coach Miranda. Her breathing now becomes heavy as she feels Miranda's hand rub over her vagina.

"Besides..." Coach Miranda then replies, "I want you to take control and dominate me. Show me exactly how your boyfriend handled you last night."

"Right now... Right here?" Sara asked.

"No honey, not here... Tonight at my condo." Coach Miranda tells her, "I'll text you my address and here is my credit card. I want you to get whatever implements your boyfriend used on you... Get whatever you need. I want to experience it all!"

Sarah's cute little smirk turns into a full smile as she takes the credit card from her coach. She watches as Coach Miranda walks over and locks the office door. She then sees her move several items to completely clear off the desk in the office. Coach Miranda returns to her and once again places her hand on Sarah's leggings and rubs gently over her vagina.

"In the meantime, I plan on taking care of all this wetness I'm feeling through your leggings." Coach Miranda says with a sexy, sarcastic tone as she continues to feel the moisture. She proceeds to pet and rub her hands over Sarah's vagina.

Sarah feels herself getting pulled as Coach Miranda walks her over to the front of the desk. She feels Miranda's hands slip under the waistband of her leggings, tugging them downward until they are gathered around her ankles. She watches as her panties quickly follow and her sneakers, socks, and clothing are removed and placed on a chair in the office.

Coach Miranda takes in the full beauty of Sarah standing completely naked in her birthday suit in front of the large desk. She escorts her up and onto the desk as her hands spread Sarah's legs open. Sarah looks down and watches Miranda's face disappear between her legs. She then feels Miranda's lips and tongue trace the wetness that's on her inner thigh upward toward her vagina. Once again, she revels in the feeling of having Miranda's lips and tongue on her skin that are so much different than her boyfriend Caleb's.

She tilts her head backward as her vagina continues to flow with wetness. She feels Coach Miranda's fingers open her lady lips as her tongue starts to lick her clitoris. Sarah instantly responds with deep breaths and soft moans that let Miranda know exactly what she's feeling. Miranda takes the cue and places her mouth completely over Sarah's vagina. She engulfs her labia and applies a gentle sucking motion along with her delicate kisses and licks. She then moves her hands upward to touch and fondle Sarah's small, perky breasts as her tongue tastes every drop of her student's juices.

Sarah's breathing became increasingly rapid from this new experience. Miranda uses her fingers to rub and then plunge into Sarah's vagina as her tongue continues to please her. Miranda takes a slight pause from licking and kissing the young student's vagina and once again engulfs her mouth into a passionate kiss. She intensifies the way her fingers are exploring Sarah's pussy and starts to plunge them even deeper into her. Sarah's gasps in response to the passionate kiss and the way Miranda's tongue tastes as she feels her fingers deep inside touching every inch of her vaginal wall.

Miranda ends the kiss with another sexy little bite. This time it's on the left side of Sarah's neck. She then removes her fingers for a moment and places them in Sarah's mouth.

"I want to show you how good you taste." She says to Sarah in a very sexy voice.

Sarah's tongue devours Miranda's fingers as she tastes her own juices. Miranda traces her tongue down Sarah's neck and all over her breasts. She pauses at each nipple and gently sucks on them before continuing to trace her tongue over Sarah's stomach and back down to her vagina. Once again, her tongue graces and licks over Sarah's clitoris.

This causes Sarah to respond with even more deep breaths and soft moans. Miranda momentarily pulls her away to just take a moment and look as her hands spread Sarah's legs as wide as possible.

"I want to see you touch yourself." Miranda tells her as she guides her student's right hand down to play with herself.

Sarah follows through and starts rubbing and petting her own vagina as Miranda watches intently. Miranda is totally turned on watching Sarah play with herself as she continues to hold her legs spread open. Sarah's wetness increases and becomes even more visible, enticing Miranda to go down and get another taste.

Miranda quickly responds and once again her tongue captures every drop of Sarah's juices. She plunges it inside her vagina to compliment Sarah's fingers that are still fingering and rubbing herself. As Miranda licks and sucks over her labia and clitoris, Sarah loses control and announces.

"I'm gonna cum!"

Miranda quickly pulls her mouth away along with Sarah's hand and instructs, "Oh no you're not… not yet. Get on all fours. I need to see that amazing ass of yours again!"

Sarah quickly moves and positions herself on all fours and then looks over her shoulder. She sees Miranda staring and admiring her body, which again plays right into her exhibitionist side perfectly. Miranda grabs the inside of Sarah's lower ass cheeks and pulls them apart as her tongue licks all over her butt and downward back over her vagina. Once again, she applies the gentle sucking pressure alternating over Sarah's labia and clitoris.

Sarah's body trembles and once again she experiences the magic of Miranda's tongue and lips all over her intimate areas. As her moans increase, it doesn't take long for her to call out again.

"Mmm… Aahh… I'm gonna cum!"

Chapter 25

This time Miranda doesn't stop her and adds to her pleasure by inserting her index finger into Sarah's rectum. Sarah feels Miranda's finger enter her and totally lets go into an amazing orgasm.

"Aah… Yes!… Mmm!"

Her body shakes and trembles as she experiences the full effect of being pleasured by her coach. Miranda keeps her tongue glued to Sarah's vagina and her finger deep inside of her butt until she's sure Sarah's orgasm is completely over. Once she's convinced, she pulls her mouth away and removes her finger as her pretty student expresses her delight.

"Phew! Oh My God!" Sarah announces as her body recovers, "That was beyond amazing!"

Coach Miranda smiles as her lips gently kiss Sarah's mouth.

"You are amazing!... That body!...You are just so beautiful." Coach replies.

Sarah climbs off the desk and embraces her coach with a warm and passionate hug. She stares into her eyes and opens up.

"This was my first experience with a woman." Sarah admits, "Thank you… You are so beautiful, so curvy and womanly... I can't wait to return the favor and get at your body."

She continues, "It's your turn to get up on the desk and let me go down on you. I may not have any experience with giving a woman oral, but I'm willing to try and I know you will guide me. I want to please you."

Coach smiles and touches her face as she stares into Sarah's big brown eyes.

"It's not like I have a lot of experience either with a girl or a woman. I had one encounter when I was your age in college and another about 2 years ago after I divorced my husband. Even though I really enjoyed the sex with her, she wasn't my type. Actually, she was a little too butch for me. It made me crave a man even more..." Coach laughs and continues, "but you... you are perfect and so pretty."

Sarah blushes and then smiles as she hears the compliments from her coach. She squats down in front of Miranda and reaches up to pull her yoga pants down. Miranda intercepts her hands and stops her.

"I'm so turned on, but let's save this for tonight. I need to get back to the tent and monitor the vaccinations." Coach tells her as she sees a disappointed look come over Sarah's face.

"I promise you, Sarah...trust me..." She reassures her, "Tonight you will have all of me and I especially want to experience the exact way your boyfriend handled you. Remember to go and buy whatever you want and I'll text you later with my address."

Sarah manages to crack a little smile through her disappointment knowing that the coach already took a huge risk to be here with her. She realizes Coach Miranda's obligations to the team and that she needs to get back and supervise.

"Fine!" Sarah says with a sexy, sarcastic attitude, "Go back and look at all the other girls bare bottoms getting their shots, but tonight I'm going to be looking at yours when I dominate and spank you!"

Sarah's young and innocent look contrasted with her total sexiness really does something to Miranda as she immediately responds.

"Oh, I can't wait... It's been a long time since someone has taken control and done that to me... I'm long overdue!"

Coach Miranda's response triggers Sarah to embrace her in another hug before letting her go to resume her duties to the team.

"And Sarah… Remember, our story is that you are dehydrated. That's what I'm telling the team and that's the reason why you are excused from practice today. Stay in here for a little bit longer to make it seem like you are resting." Coach reminds her as she walks out the door and leaves the field house.

Chapter 26

Caleb finally got going and is now clean, clothed, and freshly shaved. He grabs his phone and powers it on as he walks out of his bedroom and into his living room. Of course, he has an incredibly sexy video that his girlfriend Sarah made for him last night while he was fast asleep.

He also has a few secrets of his own, and he removes the cameras that he had hidden in his living room from last night. Sarah had no clue that while she was blindfolded and being dominated, spanked and fucked that Caleb captured every second of it. Not only does he have a video of their epic event, he has multiple cameras and multiple angles. His intention wasn't to undermine or betray Sarah's trust. It was more to surprise her and assemble a kinky video reminder that they could watch together and enjoy.

As he sits down with his morning coffee, he goes to work editing the video. It's not that hard of a task, since Sarah looks absolutely stunning from every angle that he captured. Within a few minutes of editing the video, he quickly sports another hard-on as his dick responds to everything that his eyes are seeing.

At 22 years old, Caleb's testosterone is running rampant. It doesn't take much for him to get as hard as a baseball bat. In fact, his penis seems to be in a constant state of erection, which has often contributed to the many pitfalls he's experienced, especially with his relationships. He ignores pleasuring himself right now in order to focus on compiling the video. After working diligently for about 2 hours, the video is complete. He manages to get the entire night edited down to a 20 minute action-packed, erotic masterpiece. He even mixed down the background music to enhance the sound of his leather strap connecting to her luscious ass, as well as, her yelps, and sounds of delight.

Of course, Caleb was extra careful not to show his own red ass cheeks in the video, especially when he lowered his pants and fucked her brains out. For those times, he simply zoomed in on his cock pounding her pussy into oblivion and coupled it with close-ups of her beautiful face. He also captured every nuance of the pleasure-filled sounds of approval that came out of her mouth. Her sexy moans of ecstasy sounded so good that he couldn't help but give in. He now lowered his pants and underwear and proceeded to feverishly stroke himself to another eruption.

After another clean-up, Caleb makes himself a protein shake, grabs his exercise bag, and is ready to head to the gym for a workout. He's interrupted by a knock on the door as he opens it to retrieve a package. It's the confirmation letter for his promotion at work. It details his new salary, stock options, and also contains the medical paperwork that he needs to be completed.

Caleb's excited about his new position, not to mention his incredible new salary, as a Senior Analyst. He feels that things are finally moving in a positive direction for him. Now all he has to do is stay focused and not screw things up. This is where his spanking agreement with Mrs. Doyle will really help. That is, if they can continue to keep it hidden and no one else finds out.

Caleb reaches for his phone to text his spanking neighbor. Since Mrs. Doyle is an APRN, she offered to write out the script for him to get the required blood work he needs for his employment. She also offered to give him the physical exam and the vaccines that are required as well.

Caleb composes a text to her that reads.

"Good morning, How R U? I just wanted to let you know that I received my promotion letter and medical paperwork for my new position. Are you around to review it?"

A moment later, he receives a text back from her on his phone.

"Hi Caleb, I'm great thx. I just finished my tennis lesson. I'm stopping for a few groceries. I'll be home in about 20 minutes. Stop over and I'll go thru the paperwork with you."

Twenty minutes go by quickly and Caleb sees Mrs. Doyle's car pull in to her driveway. He walks over to help her as she's about to grab a couple of grocery bags from her car. The smile he displays lights up his entire face as he looks at her and says, "Hi, I can't get those."

"Oh, Thank you, honey," she replies in her nurturing, motherly voice as she carries her gym bag and tennis racket inside while Caleb carries the grocery bags.

Once inside, she quickly puts the groceries away and then signals for them to sit down at the kitchen table.

"Can I get you anything, Sweetheart?… Coffee? Tea?" She asks.

"Maybe just a glass of water." He replies.

As Mrs. Doyle reaches for a glass and then goes to the refrigerator to fill it, Caleb's eyes quickly take in the view of her mature, athletic body. Being twice his age, her looks and physique are much different than his girlfriend Sarah's, and the young college girls that he's scored with. Mrs. Doyle is sophisticated, sexy, and all woman. The nurturing yet stern mom looks absolutely beautiful in her thin black leggings and sporty top. The clothing that she's wearing clings to all of her curves just right, especially her full ass, and shapely hips.

Caleb's eyes now focus on her big blue eyes as she hands him the water and sits down with him at the kitchen table.

"So, how are you today? How's that hiney of yours feeling?"

Her cute smirk is followed up with an equally cute giggle as she asks the question to follow up on their spanking session from yesterday.

"It's pretty sore…" Caleb chuckles along with her, "I really feel it when I sit."

"I'm sure you do," She replies, "I gave you one heck of a spanking yesterday."

Caleb smirks and responds with a bit of humor.

"You sure did, Ma'am. I guess your tennis lessons are really working because your swing is insanely powerful and accurate, I might add! There wasn't an unmarked area on my entire butt when you were done with it yesterday. Some of the marks have faded, but there's still a few good ones on it, and it's quite tender in some spots."

Caleb brazenly stands up, then turns around and lowers his sweat pants and underwear just enough to show her his rear end. It still has some prominent stripes, along with some round, purplish marks on both cheeks, thanks to her. She definitely didn't hold back yesterday when she gave him a bare bottom spanking with her thick, leather strap and wooden spoon.

"Wow, I wasn't expecting that!" Mrs. Doyle chuckles as Caleb bares his butt to her.

She can't help herself and reaches out to touch his ass. She lets her fingertips slowly and gently trace over a couple of the remaining marks. Mrs. Doyle lightly presses on a large, purplish mark and then gently pulls his ass cheeks apart to give it a thorough inspection.

Caleb turns his head over his left shoulder as he feels her fingertips touch his butt and glide over all of the marks. He winces to himself as he feels her press on the tender area before her hands proceed to spread his cheeks. He can't help but notice the way she's smiling with approval and intently staring at his ass. Her sky-blue eyes are as big as saucers and fully open as her hands slightly tighten their grip on his bare bottom. Since she's sitting down and he's standing, his rear end is totally at eye level for her and just inches from her face. This intimate interaction once again has Caleb's penis reacting as he manages to keep it covered, allowing just his marked rear end to be on display.

After a good look and fondling, Mrs Doyle comments, "I can rub some lotion on your hiney, sweetheart. It might help a little to soothe those tender areas."

Caleb responds, "Actually, I kind of like it, Ma'am. It makes me remember the spanking you gave me."

His admittance makes his pretty neighbor blush as she's obviously a bit flustered. Even though she wants to continue touching him, she releases her grip on his cheeks and gives them a gentle, loving pat.

"Well, like I said when you asked me to spank you… It's your hiney, sweetheart… And GOD… what a hiney it is! I've seen a lot of rear ends in my line of work and yours is truly spectacular. Whatever you're doing in the gym, keep doing it! It's the best butt I've ever seen on a guy."

Her humor once again makes Caleb laugh and feel relaxed as he pulls his pants and underwear up and sits back down at the kitchen table.

A bit flustered and overheated, Mrs. Doyle jokingly fans her hands over her face and says, "Whew! It got a little hot in here!

They both laugh in unison, and once she re-gains her composure, she replies, "Now, let's look at those medical forms."

Chapter 27

Mrs. Doyle slips on a pair of reading glasses as she takes a few minutes to look over all the medical forms and information that Caleb's workplace is requiring. She now has the added look of a sexy librarian with those thin frames accenting her pretty face. Caleb's entire body is tingling as he watches her go over all of the paperwork. After reading every form, she turns to Caleb and reiterates.

"So as you know, they want full blood work, drug tests, and a urine sample. I can write you out the script and you'll have to get this from a lab. As far as the physical examination and the vaccines required, you can go to a walk-in medical center, your own doctor, or I can do it… It's up to you."

Caleb already knew his answer. He can't deny the attraction he has to his beautiful neighbor, so of course he wants her to touch and examine his body. He's not proud that he's totally infatuated with his good friend Ryder's mom. Basically, he'll take any opportunity he can to have her hands on his body.

"Well, you've already seen me naked so…" Caleb gives a nonchalant reply.

"Yes, I have honey, but this is different from me spanking your bottom. I'll be fully examining you and touching every inch of your body… inside and out." She relays back to him.

Caleb replies, "Yep, I know. Can we keep this to ourselves as well?"

"Of course, sweetie." She smiles and replies, "My family and your girlfriend don't have to know. My name and medical credentials will be on your forms, but only your employer will see them. James and my kids are still away camping for a few more days, so we can do it later this afternoon or early evening, after you get your blood work done."

Caleb smiles back in agreement, "Thank you, Mrs. Doyle. I'll go now and get my lab work done. Then I'll head to the gym and do my workout. After I get home and take a shower, I'll call you. Is that okay?"

"Perfect… Here's the script you need." Mrs. Doyle replies and then asks.

"So, Caleb... How did last night go? Did Sarah like her kinky, little surprise? I take it that she didn't see your bruised bottom, right?"

"Haha, it went really well." Caleb responds with a laugh.

"She loved being dominated and I really spanked her good! Her butt looks about as marked as mine… And no, I managed to keep my butt hidden from her thanks to the blindfold and restraints."

He ends his response by flashing Mrs. Doyle his killer smile that leads into his cute laugh. Caleb then exits her house with his medical forms in hand. As he gets into his car, he can't help but think about the physical examination that Mrs. Doyle will give him later on. He formulates all kinds of kinky thoughts as his mind pictures her hands examining and touching every inch of his body. As usual, his dick is pointing straight upward and forming a tent beneath his sweat pants.

Mrs. Doyle waves goodbye and watches as Caleb walks back to his car and then pulls away. Her hand quickly slides over her exercise pants as she starts rubbing her vagina. Everything that Caleb is feeling, Megan Doyle is feeling also, and maybe even more. She just had his ass cheeks in her hands as she looked over the marks her strap made on them yesterday. Now, it will only be a few more hours until she sees him completely naked and gives him a full physical examination. This is a legitimate reason to touch and fondle his testicles and penis. She also can't wait to examine and plunge her index finger deep into his rectum. The mere thought of this has her vagina flowing with moisture as her hand continues to rub in small circles.

She retreats to her bedroom, removes her leggings, grabs her vibrator, and lays on her bed. She closes her eyes as she once again fantasizes over her young neighbor. Within a minute of having the vibrator tingle her clitoris, her body shakes vigorously and she experiences relief and savors an intense orgasm.

As Caleb drives to the lab, his dick is practically holding the steering wheel. He calls his girlfriend to check in and also to make sure that she doesn't come by and find him over at Mrs. Doyle's later getting his physical exam.

Sarah answers, "Hey babe, what's' up?"

"Not much, just checking in. How are you? Is practice over?"

"Ummm… yeah, it's good... Ummm yeah…" Sarah's voice sounds frazzled as she continues.

"Got my vaccine... and Ummm… Coach Miranda wants me to take in a lot of water, Gatorade, and rest. She excused me from practice today. It seems I'm a bit dehydrated and run down, so I need to take a rain check on getting together tonight. I'm just going to chill out and get to bed early. I guess a certain someone had me up way too late last night."

Of course, that was a great way for her to cover-up the fact that she plans on going over to Coach Miranda's condo and totally dominating her.

Caleb slightly giggles and responds back, "Sure babe, I won't call you and I'll let you rest. I have a lot to do this afternoon that will take me into the evening. All the forms just got delivered for my new job, so I'm driving into the city to get my blood work done. Then I have to go to the walk-in medical center for my physical exam and vaccines. I'm going to be a while and I probably won't be back until later tonight, but that will be the perfect time for me to watch that little video you made me."

Sarah giggles and responds, "Haha, enjoy it babe. I'll text in the morning when I wake up."

Of course, Caleb fails to tell her that his hot spanking neighbor will be the one probing every inch of his body and giving him the physical exam. Sarah thinks nothing of it and they both agree to take the night off from seeing each other. They end their conversation with plans to check in and talk in the morning.

Once again, Caleb feels a decent amount of guilt from not telling Sarah the complete truth. However, he quickly gets over it as his mind focuses back on Mrs. Doyle, their spanking agreement, and his upcoming physical.

As he continues to drive, his mind fantasizes about his night with her. Maybe he should be uncooperative and misbehave during his physical. That would surely give her another reason to get at his rear end and spank him. He also vividly pictures bending her over the exam table, grabbing onto her nice wide hips, and forcefully ramming his dick deep into her.

As much as Caleb is into his girlfriend Sarah, he also has it really bad for Mrs. Doyle. There's just something so sexy and so appealing that it makes him constantly fantasize about her. Maybe it's her mature and sophisticated vibe that compliments that beautiful, curvy body of hers. Maybe it's her warm, loving nature that can easily turn at the drop of a dime into a stern, no-nonsense mom that doesn't hesitate to pull pants down and correct naughty behavior with her leather strap. Whatever it is, all Caleb has to do is think about her and his penis instantly rises into a stiff, hard-on.

Caleb is also well aware of the countless compliments Mrs. Doyle gives him about his looks and his physique. He knows from her own admission that she's also enjoying this kinky arrangement and bond they've established. Mrs. Doyle totally came clean, confessing to Caleb, that she's been unsatisfied and bored with her husband and his lack of sexual creativity. Caleb knows that her vanilla husband can never excite her the way he can. So this spanking arrangement isn't just good for Caleb, it's also filling a void in her as well. It might just be the added kink and excitement that's missing in her life.

Caleb arrives at the location and proceeds to get his lab work done. He then drives to the gym and puts in a killer workout that lasts about 2 hours. As he drives back home he has plenty of time to think and fantasize about his physical with Mrs. Doyle. His dick is once again rock hard from the very thought of everything.

As the sun vanishes and the skies fade into dusk, he arrives home. He heads straight into the shower and gets himself squeaky clean. It took everything he had to resist the urge to stroke and relieve himself of his erection. Besides, if Mrs. Doyle is going to see and examine him, she might as well see him at his best. Caleb's kinky mind explodes with thoughts as his anticipation gets his heart beating in double time.

He reaches out to his neighbor with a quick text.

"Hi... I'm just checking in. Are you ready for my physical?"

Mrs. Doyle quickly responds in a text back to him.
"I sure am!"

Chapter 28

Caleb walks over to her house and rings the doorbell. Mrs. Doyle opens it and greets him with a pearly, white smile.

"Hi honey, come on in. We'll go downstairs to my office."

She leads the way to the lower level of her home. Caleb's eyes can't help but focus on the way her ass cheeks gently shake underneath the thin fabric of her pretty sundress. They enter the area of her home where she works and sees patients. She gives Caleb a quick tour of the room.

"This is where I teach online nursing classes and have Zoom meetings." She tells him as she points to the area of the large room that has her desk, computer, and some filing cabinets.

"And this is where I work and see patients." She then points out the area of the room with an exam table, various counters with canisters and supplies, a separate bathroom, and a changing area.

Caleb's dick is already throbbing beneath his jeans as his eyes take in the room, as well as, his beautiful neighbor. His nose takes in the scent of her skin that's freshly coated with a flowery fragrance. He tries to shrug off a bit of nervous energy as the shivers run up and down his spine.

"Nervous?" She asks.

"Yeah, a little... And of course, a bit excited, as you probably already know." He replies.

His slight trepidation and innocent half smile makes her reach for his hand. She takes a hold of it in her loving, nurturing way and walks him over to the changing room.

"I understand, sweetheart. I'll do my best to make this easy and help you relax. It's just you and I, we can take our time. This is the changing room. All clothing comes off except for your underwear. There's a gown in that closet if you want to be slightly covered."

She gives him a gentle, little pat on his bottom over his jeans before releasing his hand. Caleb smiles back at her, then haphazardly giggles. "I think we're way beyond that, Ma'am. You've already seen all of me, so I won't need the gown."

As Caleb is in the changing room, Mrs. Doyle stands at the far end of the room behind the exam table. Hidden from his view, she reaches her hand underneath her sundress. She already feels the wetness in her panties as she lets her fingers gently rub over her vagina. When she hears the door of the changing room open, her hand quickly retreats from touching herself. Caleb now walks out of the changing room wearing just his thin, athletic, boxer-style, underwear. The fabric clings so well to his lower body that it's almost like a second skin. It fits tightly around his muscular legs, and perfectly frames his nice, round ass.

Mrs. Doyle's knees buckle as her eyes take in the sight of Caleb emerging from the changing room in just his underwear. Her heart skips a beat, then flutters rapidly as her vagina tingles in anticipation of examining his body. His physique is about as perfect as there is, with his broad shoulders, and V-shaped torso that flows down to a small waist. His abs are defined nicely as they ripple with his every move. His legs are also nicely sculpted, and very muscular but not overdone like the freakish, steroid-popping, bodybuilders of today. And of course, his cute ass and that well-endowed penis of his are just a thing of beauty. It makes Megan Doyle gush and drives her completely wild.

She loved every second of aggressively handling him, stripping his clothing off, and delivering her leather strap to that amazing rear end of his yesterday. The feeling of power, control, and authority isn't new for her since she's used to spanking and disciplining her own kids, but with Caleb is was completely different. There was an added amount of sexual energy that she wasn't expecting when she agreed to spank him. Now here she is, trying her best to ignore the wetness that's accumulating in her panties. Her beautiful, blue eyes open widely as she continues to look his body over. She then flashes that cute smile of hers and signals with her right hand for him to walk toward her while she points with her left hand for him to step on the scale.

"First, we'll get your weight. Go ahead and step on the scale, honey." She tells him.

Caleb absolutely loves all the terms of endearment that she uses when she talks to him. It seems she's always calling him honey, sweetheart, or cutie. He didn't need anything else to rev up his engine, but her warm vocal tone sure makes his penis throb. And then, in total contrast, there's that stern voice that she uses when dishing out a spanking. That get-down-to-business side of her just drives him completely wild. His mind gets carried away for a second as he reflects on the way she delivered her leather strap to his behind yesterday. He quickly snaps out of it when he feels her hand touch the small of his back to guide him up on the scale. Caleb gets the shivers as he feels her fingers on his skin. He then proceeds and steps up on the scale, puts his arms down at his sides, and looks straight ahead at the digital display.

Mrs. Doyle stands slightly behind him, and once again, she inconspicuously slides her hand under her dress and sneaks another quick touch to her panties. After a quick rub, she retracts her hand and reads out loud "181.4."

Caleb jokingly responds, "Really? I thought I was under 180. It must be the ton of late night ice cream I've eaten over the last several days. There's nothing better after…"

He catches himself and stops before he finishes his sentence, to which Mrs. Doyle easily fills in the blanks.

"You mean after sex." She laughs. "You're right, there isn't anything better than ice cream after that!"

"Well, as you know, the last several days have been a complete whirlwind for me… Actually, life changing! Ever since I witnessed that stern side of you come out. The way you handled your son, pulled his pants down, and spanked him in my garage... right before my eyes! I'm being completely honest and open when I tell you that it's really awakened something in me."

Mrs. Doyle takes her clipboard and writes down Caleb's body weight. She then smirks and responds,
"Yep, seems like that was the catalyst for your sudden interest in all things spanking. From the websites and videos you shared with me, to the implements you purchased and used on Sarah last night. It's crazy that it all started with you seeing me discipline Dillon. Oh, and lets not forget, it's also the reason you have a marked and tender hiney right now."

Mrs. Doyle ends with her sarcastic but really cute laugh. Caleb lets out a little chuckle as her quirky humor makes her even more desirable to him. He turns his head to the side to make eye contact with her as he replies.

"Yes, it was the catalyst... I feel a totally different energy inside me... especially sexually!"

"So no regrets?" She asks.

"Regrets? No... Why?" He replies.

"Well, I just want to make sure. It's not everyday a guy gets forcefully exposed and spanked by their next-door neighbor, especially when it's their good friend's mom.

"I can assure you, Mrs. Doyle, I have zero regrets. Some guilt... yeah, because I have a girlfriend... but no regrets at all. I got away with everything growing up, and I still do at times. My dad was always working and my mom was just way too lenient. When I witnessed that strict side of you and the way you corrected your son's attitude by spanking him, I realized that type of discipline and accountability was, and is, missing in my life. Right then and there, I knew that I needed to experience that exact spanking. And man... you are fierce... you didn't hold back one bit!" Caleb replies as he places his hands over his underwear and touches his butt, signaling how sore it is.

Mrs. Doyle displays that sexy, trademark smirk of hers and then replies with a cute giggle, "Well, you wanted me to discipline you the way I do my own kids, and that's exactly what I did... but actually, even harder. When they misbehave, their pants come down, and my leather strap comes out. I may be a young mom, but I'm very old-fashion, and I'll never tolerate my kids being disrespectful or disobedient. So you're right, if it gets to that point, I do not hold back."

Once again, this open and honest dialog further builds upon the bond and trust they've established over the last couple of days. Right from the start, their conversations seemed to flow effortlessly as they talked about past relationships, spanking, and even sex. This type of nothing-is-off-limits, communication is something that really drew Mrs. Doyle into her young neighbor. She totally understood his reasoning, and his need for discipline. In fact, she actually related to it from her own personal experience. It was very similar to the way she felt in college and the spanking relationship that she had with one of her professors, Mr. Roberts.

Maybe this was the reason that she agreed to spank Caleb, and also hold him accountable for future misdemeanors. Or maybe it's because he's just so damn hot! Either way, here she is, getting incredibly wet as she's looking him up and down, standing there in his underwear. Caleb wasn't the only one that had something awakened deep inside from that spanking. It also stirred up some sexual energy that's been dormant in Megan Doyle for years. Right now she's using all the willpower she has not to act on it as her mind is racing with the thoughts of just fucking his brains out.

Mrs. Doyle manages to regain her focus and tackle the task at hand of giving him his physical examination.

"Anyway, let me double check the scale and make sure it's properly calibrated. Step off it for a second, honey."

Caleb steps off the scale and watches as Mrs. Doyle proceeds to re-calibrate by resetting the scale to zero. She then comments, "There, now it's set back to zero. Let's try this again and we'll make one other adjustment to make sure your body weight is completely accurate."

Without any hesitation, and in the blink of an eye, she slips her fingers inside the waistband of Caleb's underwear and quickly tugs them down to the floor. Caleb wasn't expecting that at all, as her bold move took him by surprise. It's the same no-hesitation way she pulled his pants down yesterday and introduced her leather strap to his bare bottom. This assertive act alone gets a rise out of him and turns him on beyond belief. As his underwear gathers around his ankles, he feels his penis respond to a full-fledged erection.

"Step out of them, sweetheart." She says as she gets that little twinkle in her eyes.

Chapter 29

Caleb follows through and steps completely out of his underwear. He stands right there before her in his birthday suit complete with a huge hard-on.

"I already knew this was going to happen." Caleb admits as he looks down at his fully erect penis.

"That penis of yours is really good for my ego, Caleb." She smiles as her eyes continue to take in every inch of it.

Caleb lifts his eyes from staring at his own dick to now focus on her smiling face as he replies.

"I'm sorry, Ma'am, but you're just so attractive and so sexy. Especially when that bold, assertive, side of you comes out. It would be impossible for any guy not to react this way. I've already admitted that I feel this new sexual energy in me. It's all because of you and I can't help it. I guess my hormones are just out of control right now."

Mrs. Doyle's face lights up even more as her cheeks blush with a slight redness from his compliment.

"Thank you, honey." She replies, "You're not the only one that feels a new energy. I haven't felt this sexually awake in years. My hormones are raging as well, and let's just say I have this tingling in certain areas of my body right now."

Caleb's doing all he can to refrain from ripping her clothes off and pounding her into oblivion the way he does all the college girls he fucks. Instead, he politely asks, "Should we stop this physical?"

"Are you out of your mind?" She quickly replies, "Fuck no! I love this feeling! And since you like seeing the stern side of me..."

<SLAP>

She raises her voice.

"Get your cute ass back on that scale, mister!"

<SLAP><SLAP>

Mrs. Doyle delivers several quick, open hand, spanks with full force to his already tender butt. Caleb wasn't expecting that at all as his body naturally tucks inward from the sting of her palm.

"God, I love that! That's definitely not going to help make my erection go down." He jokes.

"Then, maybe I need to get the wooden spoon." She replies, as she opens a drawer in her desk and retrieves a large, wooden spoon.

"Here we go!" She announces as she taps the wooden spoon several times, in the palm of her hand.

"Along with a strap, this is one of a mom's best friends." She chuckles, "I keep this down here in my office, because many times I discipline my kids down here, especially Dillon. Jim hates to hear it when I give him a spanking and he bawls his eyes out. I swear, my husband is such a wimp!... So, at least my office here on the lower level, is great for that purpose. It's far enough away from the rest of the house, and Jim doesn't hear much at all."

"Well, I can vouch for feeling the full sting of your spoon. I didn't cry my eyes out yesterday, but I sure yelped a lot." Caleb smirks.

Mrs. Doyle approached him with her wooden spoon, as her eyes cast a glare on his cute, round bottom.
"I'll keep this close by in case you misbehave." She smirks, and then watches as his Greek God-like body steps back on the scale.

"181.3" She laughs, "Is that better?"

Caleb laughs as he feels her take his arm and lead her to the exam table. She motions for him to sit as she gets her stethoscope, places it over her ears, and then holds the end of it on his muscular chest, over his heart.

"Take a deep breath, sweetheart." She instructs as she proceeds to listen to his heartbeat.

She moves the stethoscope over several areas of his chest and then proceeds to do the same on his back. Caleb feels the cold metal tip on his body, as well as, the contrast to the warmth of her fingers.

"Does everything sound okay?" He asks.

"Oh, everything sounds and looks perfect!" She replies with a flirty tone as her eyes take in the sight of his toned chest and then once again, glare down at his penis.

"God, that's just beautiful!" She replies, and then moves forward with the usual procedures of checking his pulse, ears, tonsils, feeling his throat, getting his blood pressure, and oxygen level.

Hearing that comment she made about his penis and feeling her fingers on his body are absolutely driving Caleb mad. He can't take his eyes off of her as he watches her every move, examining his body.

She now grabs a digital thermometer and swipes it across his forehead.

"Your temperature is perfect, as well as your oxygen and blood pressure.

Caleb decides to flirt with a witty remark.
"I guess you're not really that old-fashion if you're taking my temperature that way."

"Haha..." Mrs. Doyle laughs at his wise ass comment.
"You're right, honey. What was I thinking?"

"Lay flat on your tummy, hiney up, and I'll get my other thermometer."

Caleb's sly remark works as he maneuvers himself into a position lying flat on his stomach. He lifts his head slightly to watch as Mrs. Doyle retrieves the older style thermometer. His eyes once again watch her every move as she places the tip of it in Vaseline, and then continues to rub more on it with her fingers.

She walks back over to her exam table with the jar of Vaseline in her hand. She then positions herself slightly behind him and off his left side. Her eyes take in another lovely sight as she looks down at his perfectly round rear-end.

"God, I love this view also!" She admits as her hands take hold of his ass cheeks.

"Relax, honey." She instructs as she spreads his cheeks and holds them open.

He feels her fingertip slightly enter his anus as she dabs some additional Vaseline in and around it. Caleb manages to hold in his gasp as he feels her fingertip graze inside his rectum. He's turned on so much that it's a wonder he hasn't cum all over the table.

"Okay, sweetheart… Deep breath." She instructs as she touches the thermometer to his opening.

Caleb takes a deep breath in as he feels her push the thermometer into his rectum.

Mrs. Doyle's right hand remains holding the end of the thermometer as her left hand gently pats his rear-end.

"Squeeze your cheeks for me and hold it in there, honey." She tells him as her hand continues to trace and further inspect the marks on his bottom.

Mrs. Doyle watches as Caleb squeezes that tight ass of his. She leaves her left hand on his left butt cheek as she then conveniently removes her right hand from holding the thermometer. Once again, she slides her hand under her sundress and rubs her vagina over her silk panties. The fabric is now totally soaked with her wetness as she inconspicuously continues to touch herself.

Caleb purposelessly turns his head to his left side and attempts to ask her a question. Mrs. Doyle quickly removes her right hand from underneath her skirt and gently taps and rubs his bottom.

"Almost done, honey. This is the old mercury-type thermometer, it takes a few minutes." She explains, and then she places her hand back on the thermometer.

Her quick action allowed her to cover her tracks as Caleb had no idea where her hand just was.

"I'm sorry, were you about to say something?" She asks.

"No problem.... I was…" He laughs. "But, when I felt your hand gently rub my butt, I totally forgot what I was going to ask you."

Caleb continues to laugh, which makes Mrs. Doyle also giggle and respond.

"Yeah, I guess that is quite a contrast to the way my hand has felt on your tush. See, I'm capable of being gentle as well. After all, I do have a very romantic side of me."

Caleb smiles to himself as he now feels her hands separate his cheeks and proceeds to pull the thermometer out.

Mrs. Doyle reads the thermometer and announces, "Well, the good news is that your temperature is normal. The bad news is..." She pauses for a moment to build up tension.

Caleb responds, "Bad news?"

She replies, "Yep, the bad news is that your temperature is normal. So I guess that means my play time with this rectal thermometer is over… Darn! I really liked doing that!"

She jokes and continues.

"It's not everyday that I have a hot, athletic, guy on my exam table needing his temperature taken rectally."

Her quirky humor once again makes them both laugh in unison, carrying on like grammar school kids. Mrs. Doyle stands over him and just takes a moment to enjoy the sight of his amazing ass. She just can't keep her hands off of it, so once again she rubs his cheeks gently, then adds a few good squeezes, and some additional pats.

"God, this ass of yours, Caleb, is just perfect. Like I was just saying... it's not everyday that I have a hot, muscular young man in this position, so there's no way that I should waste this opportunity."

Without giving it another thought, Mrs. Doyle raises her right hand high and delivers an intense sequence of slaps to his already tender bottom.

These hard, stinging, slaps took Caleb totally by surprise, especially since he was just experiencing and quite enjoying the feel of her soft, gentle touches. Since his bottom is still sore in various spots, it doesn't take much for him to respond.

"Ow!… Ouch! What did I do?" He quickly moves his right hand behind him in an attempt to cover his butt, and block her spanks.

"Oh, no you don't!" Mrs. Doyle responds, and uses her left hand to forcefully pin his arm to his lower back. Then continues to add a fresh, new shade of red to his bare bottom.

<SLAP><SLAP><SLAP>
<SLAP><SLAP>

Caleb responds, "Ouch!… Ooh!"

"You didn't do anything wrong, sweetheart." Mrs. Doyle admits, and continues to spank him.

"I just wanted to remind you..."

<SLAP><SLAP><SLAP>

"... That even though you got a taste of my soft and gentle side, there's still this stern side of me that will redden your hiney at the drop of a dime."

That strict tone in her voice penetrates Caleb's ears and makes his dick throb even more as his beautiful neighbor once again gets assertive and profusely spanks him. Mrs. Doyle expertly delivers slap after slap that instantly makes Caleb's cheeks turn colors as she firmly holds him in place.

Caleb usually has a high pain tolerance, but since she already did a number on his rear end yesterday with her leather strap, he can't help but express how painful this hand spanking feels right now.

"Ooh! Oow!" Those words coming from his mouth are music to her ears, and the confirmation she wants that he's feeling every single one of her slaps.

Mrs. Doyle has him right where she wants him, lying on her exam table, flat on his stomach, with his right arm pinned behind his back. That cute hiney of his looks even more adorable to her as she watches it involuntarily shake and quiver from her relentless slaps.

<SLAP><SLAP><SLAP><SLAP>

"OUCH!"

Even though he's expressing the pain he's feeling, Caleb, absolutely loves this power dynamic and the way she excels in this position of authority. His rear end is on fire and totally stinging from her intense slaps. He tightens and squeezes his ass cheeks as a natural reaction and an attempt to ease the pain.

<SLAP>SLAP>

"Ouch! Oow!"

Mrs. Doyle's eyes light to a greater extent as she sees Caleb clenching his ass. His round, muscular cheeks look like two melons as they pop out even more when he tightens and squeezes them together. Her vagina is so wet right now that it's totally soaking her panties. Caleb's bare bottom is something that turns Megan Doyle on more than she ever thought was possible. Her eyes can't get enough as she continues to stare intently and focus on it like a laser beam, while her hand administers more slaps.

<SLAP><SLAP>

She scolds him in a sarcastic yet sexy way.

"Oh, you can squeeze that cute coolie of yours all you want, my dear… it's not going to help!"

<SLAP><SLAP><SLAP>

Caleb continues to feel her hand blaze his bare bottom as he takes in the way she scolds him. That sardonic tone and all those old fashion words she uses to refer to his ass really make his dick tingle. This will surely be another spanking from Mrs. Doyle that he will never forget. The way she spanks him has definitely awakened something deep inside of him that constantly makes him think of her. Everything about his sexy, older neighbor makes his penis extend to epic proportions. Her age, her sophistication, her stern side, coupled with that pretty face of hers and that mature, curvy body of hers makes him putty in her hands.

To the same degree, if Megan Doyle didn't realize it before, she sure realizes it now. The truth is that she loves spanking her young neighbor, Caleb, way too much… And why wouldn't she? After 24 years of marriage that's now dull, boring, and lacking any creativity, coupled with the demands of raising two teenagers, this gives her the perfect escape. It's something exciting, new, and of course, it turns her on.

She knows that her personality is that of the controlling type. And lord knows that she loves being in a position of authority. Add all that together with an absolutely gorgeous young man that has the body of a Greek God, and it's not rocket science. This young man, who's half her age, and just a few years older than her 19-year-old son, makes her feel vibrantly sexy and alive. To make matters even worse, Caleb and her have amazing conversations that are honest and genuine. They can talk about sex, spanking, relationships, and anything else. There is also this undeniable chemistry that they have. Megan knows that Caleb finds her sexy and desirable. That feeling is something that has been missing in her life for years now, so it's not hard to understand that she's attracted to him as well.

Even though she has Caleb secured in place with his arm pinned behind his back, he manages to turn his head over his left shoulder to get a view of her spanking him. He absolutely loves the way she looks with that furrowed expression happening between her eyebrows and her big, blue eyes totally glued to his bare bottom. The pursing of her lips and that stern look of a woman on a mission, is a total turn on for him. When she gets like this, that mission of hers is simple... all she wants to do is redden a bare hiney by administering a serious spanking.

Caleb's bottom is on fire once again from the slaps of her hand raining down on it. After delivering one last flurry to make sure that she covered any white area that was remaining on his cheeks, she stops spanking him.

"There! That should do it!" She says in that sarcastic, strict voice of hers.

She pauses to give his bare bottom a good look and then lets her hand touch and squeeze it.

"Now that's what I call a good hand spanking." She announces as she continues to fondle him and feels the heat coming off his rear end.

Mrs. Doyle then walks over to her supply and reaches for a latex glove. She looks over her shoulder and smiles back at him.

"Now, that I've got that over with, it's time for your rectal exam."

Chapter 30

Caleb looks up and takes in the sight of this beautiful woman snapping a latex glove over her right hand. She stands in front of him and spreads a generous amount of Vaseline onto her gloved index finger before returning to her position on the left side of the exam table.

"Okay, sweetheart. I need you to roll over onto your left side, and lift your legs up as high as possible, in the fetal position."

Caleb's heart flutters as he anticipates her finger plunging deep into his rectum. He maneuvers himself into the position she asked him to. He's now lying on his side, facing the wall, and can't see her at all. He gets a reminder that she's right there behind him, as he feels her left hand firmly grip his right butt cheek. She then spreads and pulls it upward as her right finger gently touches his anus.

"Okay, breathe in deep, dear." Mrs. Doyle coaches him as her right finger continues to fully explore his rectum.

Caleb's dick is as hard as it's ever been in his entire life. His erection right now is literally something that would earn him big bucks in the porn industry. Mrs. Doyle's eyes can't help but take in the view of his amazing penis as she stands over him. She calls out another instruction for him to follow.

"Okay, honey, take a deep breath and hold it."

She waits for Caleb to follow through and take a deep breath. Once he begins to inhale, she plunges her finger deeper inside of him to thoroughly feel his prostate. Caleb let out a soft gasping moan.

"I'm sorry, am I hurting you, honey?" She asks in her loving and nurturing way.

"No, just the opposite, Ma'am. It's turning me on so much." He willingly admits.

Mrs. Doyle can't help but smile from his comment, as she now held her finger as deep inside of him as it could go. She then flicks the tip of it from side to side, causing him to let out another sexy moan.

"I love that we both feel comfortable enough with each other to have this open and honest communication. If it's any consolation, sweetie, doing this to you is turning me on also… Big time!" She admits back to him.

Mrs. Doyle is doing everything she can to not reach down, grab his dick, and blow him into eternity. She is dying to put his cock in her mouth, and then jump on him like a horse and ride him into the sunset. Caleb's mind is completely blown as he has his own kinky thoughts running through his head. He contemplates just going for it and making a move on her.

Mrs. Doyle manages to keep her composure, at least for now, as she completes his prostate exam and removes her finger from inside of him. She discards the latex glove, walks back over to the table, and positions herself right behind him again. Caleb's still lying on his left side, and facing the wall, not knowing exactly where she is. He wants to make a move, but isn't quite sure what to do, so he reaches back with his right hand, in an attempt to feel for her.

He manages to have his finger grace over the silky, sundress, and touch the side of her curvy hip.

Mrs. Doyle feels his touch for the first time and loves it, but she decides to have a little fun with him. She sternly calls him out. "Caleb Wynn! Are you misbehaving?"

"No Ma'am, I'm… Ummm… Ummm... just wanted to see if you were still behind me." He tries to offer a weak excuse.

"Well, I'm going to show you how I handle naughty boys that try and grab the nurse! You wanted me to discipline you the way I do my own kids, so in that case, I'm going to show you a move I use when I have them in this same position that you are in."

Mrs. Doyle takes her left hand, and grabs a hold of Caleb's right butt cheek. She makes sure to grab onto the meatiest part, and then she digs her nails into it. Caleb, instantly feels the force of her pinch as the fingernails of all five of her fingers digs into his hiney.

<PINCH>

He immediately yelps and can't help but tense up, and stay frozen in place, similar to when someone is getting their earlobe pulled. The force of her pinch, along with the sharpness of her fingernails, feels like five needles are piercing his rear-end.

"OOOw!" He lets out a whine.

Mrs. Doyle then grabs her wooden spoon, and delivers several hard swats to that same cheek, right below where her hand is holding him.

<PINCH>
<CRACK><SMACK><CRACK><SMACK><SMACK>

Caleb loudly reacts as he feels the sting of her wooden spoon, along with the force of her pinch, assaulting his bare bottom.

"OUCH!... "OOO!"

"That's right, young man! Let it out!... It lets me know that I'm doing my job... I'm gonna concentrate on one cheek at a time!" She scolds him as the wooden spoon adds a fresh new layer of red to his skin.

<PINCH>
<SMACK><WHACK><SMACK>

Caleb continues to respond as he now feels her hand repeat the same procedure on his left ass cheek.

"Oow!... OUCH!"

<PINCH>

Mrs. Doyle takes a more than firm grip, and once again her fingernails plunge into his fleshy cheek. Her eyes now focus on the left cheek of his hiney, as she makes the wooden spoon connect right below where she's pinching him.

<CRACK><WHACK><SMACK>

"OOH!" Caleb yelps again as he feels the combination of pinches and spanks.

He squeezes his butt cheeks so tight from the pain that he's feeling, that it's actually turning her on even more. She smirks, and continues to hold him securely on his side, raises the spoon high, and delivers one last round to his left cheek.

<PINCH>
<WHACK><SMACK><SMACK><CRACK>

Megan Doyle is in deep, and she knows it. Spanking and aggressively handling Caleb, has ignited a firestorm of sexual energy in her that's been buried for years.

"There!… Now that's how I handle naughty boys!" She sarcastically comments.

Caleb's dick is so hard right now that it's about to punch a hole in the wall. That stern side of her really gets his motor running.

Mrs. Doyle finally lets go of that killer hold she had on his hiney, and stops spanking him. She nonchalantly walks away to read and double checks his medical paperwork. She goes right back to business and resumes his physical.

"Okay, according to your medical records, you're fully vaccinated and all set with the COVID vaccine… And I can see here that you already had chicken pox as a kid. You're too young for the Shingles vaccine, so none of this applies."

Mrs. Doyle pays attention to every detail as she goes through and checks all the appropriate boxes on his medical forms.

"Ah, it seems your company is recommending a flu shot, but I don't think that's necessary for you. However, according to your records, it's been over 10 years since you had a tetanus shot. This I would highly recommend since you're always in the gym and very active." She relays this to him.

"Where the hell did you learn that move from?" Caleb questions as he rubs his bottom in an attempt to sooth the pain.

"Haha!" She laughs, and jokes back. "That's all mine. I invented it! As a mom, you have to do whatever you can to deliver a good spanking to your kids. Of course, they naturally squirm, try to resist, and block my spanks… So, I have some moves up my sleeve to make sure their hineys get exactly what they deserve if they misbehave."

"Holy shit!" Caleb responds as he continues to rub his bottom.

Caleb's eyes follow her closely as she goes over and prepares a syringe for his injection. She then walks back over with a smirk and instructs him.

"Okay, roll back over on your tummy, my dear. This shot is going in that sore hiney of yours."

Caleb rolls back onto his stomach, looks straight ahead, and anticipates the injection. Mrs. Doyle takes a moment once again to just stare and admire his cute bottom. She then allows her hand to slip under her dress, and this time she slips it under her panties, and plunges her fingers into her vagina. She's so turned on and it feels so good that she can almost orgasm immediately. She catches herself and once again proceeds and moves forward with completing the injection.

The scent of rubbing alcohol fills the air as she opens up a cleansing wipe. Caleb feels her swipe his right ass cheek with the alcohol pad over the area that she's about to inject. He then feels her fingers pinch a small area of his butt as she announces.

"Here we go… A little pinch…"

Mrs. Doyle proceeds to give Caleb the injection.

"Ouch!" Emanates from his mouth as he feels the needle pierce his tender right butt cheek.

"All done." She calls out.

"You can go ahead and flip back over onto your back. There's only one thing left to examine." She smiles at him as he gets into the position she requested.

His dick is still so erect that it's extending past his belly button. This causes Mrs. Doyle to look down at him with that cute but devilish type of smile of hers. She doesn't say a word, and simply cups his right testicle in her hand. She applies a bit of pressure as she fondles and squeezes it.

"Turn your head, and cough, honey." She instructs.

Caleb manages to cough through his labored breathing and panting.

Mrs. Doyle repeats the same procedure as her hand gently takes hold of his left testicle. Caleb is so turned on that he's afraid he might cum. Her hands feel like heaven as she gently applies pressure on his testicles.

"Cough for me." She instructs as her hands continue to examine his privates.

She then takes both testicles in her hand and repeats.

"One last cough, honey."

Caleb obeys and gives one last cough.

After giving him a good squeeze, Mrs. Doyle pulls her hands away. He surprises himself that he managed to complete the exam without further embarrassing himself by shooting his sperm all over her hand. His eyes look up and lock onto hers as she continues to look down and flash him that killer smile of hers.

Caleb's mind is racing and all he can think about is fucking her brains out. He finally has enough guts and he feels this is the perfect time to make his move.

Chapter 31

Caleb is more than ready, and just as he reaches out his arm to grab her, his phone rings and interrupts the moment. Mrs. Doyle reaches for his phone, since it's only a few steps away from her in the changing room, and hands it to him.

"Here you go. You can answer it, honey. I'll take a moment to complete your forms." She tells him in a flustered tone.

He answers his phone and the conversation takes less than a minute. He sits up on her exam table, still as hard as a rock, and turns to her.

"Thank you, it was just some friends wanting to get together tonight to celebrate my promotion."

Mrs. Doyle is obviously flustered and still overheated as she smiles at Caleb sitting on her exam table. Her eyes went right back down to staring at his totally erect cock.

I recommend that you go home and take care of that first, sweetheart." She tells him as she points to his dick, and then waves her own hand in front of her face to cool herself off.

"Phew! I need to cool off myself and take care of something that I'm feeling as well." She admits.

Caleb chuckles, and then asks, "Spanking me really turns you on... Doesn't it?"

"It sure does, my dear, but you already knew that. You have a way of really revving up my adrenaline and bringing out this naughty side of me." She smiles.

"Well, lucky for you, that I know just how to handle naughty girls. You're not the only one that can give a good spanking." Caleb responds and then looks down and starts scrolling through his cell phone.

She raises her eyebrows with a look of disbelief and then responds, using her sarcasm. "It's been a long time since someone put me in my place, and spanked this ass of mine."

Caleb taps the screen of his phone and then holds it up, forcing Mrs. Doyle to take a look. Mrs. Doyle's eyes nearly pop out of her head and she stops in her tracks. She then grabs the phone from his hand to take a closer look at the action on the screen. Caleb has his phone playing a video clip that he made from dominating his girlfriend, Sarah, last night. The video shows Sarah completely naked, tied, and blindfolded in Caleb's living room. It then shows Caleb aggressively handling her and delivering swat after intense swat with his thick leather strap to her beautiful ass.

Mrs. Doyle watches in amazement as Caleb not only looks incredibly sexy, he also has the perfect attitude and skill set, to pull off being in this position of authority. He's really taking charge, scolding Sarah, grabbing her, and using force as she squirms, struggles, and tries to resist being spanked.

"Holy Fuck! I LOVE THIS! Show me more!" She excitedly replies to Caleb, and then hands the phone back to him.

Caleb then fast forwards the video to a scene that really has Sarah moaning and dancing from leg to leg from the stripes he's putting across her cheeks with that leather strap. He then skips forward to another part of the video that shows him manhandling and forcefully holding Sarah in place over his knee. It then gets even more impressive when he quickly locks his strong, muscular legs over both of hers.

"She's a feisty one, as you can see, so I made sure she couldn't struggle or get away!" He tells Mrs. Doyle with his own confident smirk.

Mrs. Doyle's eyes really lit up seeing Caleb administer this hand-spanking without holding back. He's really delivering intense slaps to his girlfriend's ass that have her bawling her eyes out. Caleb then skips to another part of the video where he puts Sarah flat on her back, and lifts her legs up, in the diaper position.

"See this move..." He flirts with Mrs. Doyle. "I learned this move from a very hot, very stern neighbor, that gave me the spanking of my life!"

"Nice move, Caleb!" Mrs. Doyle flashes him that sexy smirk, and keeps her eyes glued to his screen.

Mrs. Doyle is turned on to the point of craziness as she continues to watch the video. It goes on to show Caleb administer a truly, relentless hand-spanking that makes Sarah cry a river, and use her safe word.

"Wow! Wow! Wow!, Caleb!" Mrs. Doyle comments.

It's about all that she can manage to say as she's tingling inside and out. She's simply dumbfounded by that video and the way that Caleb took control, and dished out the discipline. She can't believe that this sexy and dominant man she just watched on video, lives right next door to her.

This can't be the same young man that she strapped and punished like her own kids a days ago in his garage... But it is!... And, she just finished spanking him again, and even gave him a thorough physical. So here he is, right before her eyes, sitting up on her exam table, with that beautiful dick that's as hard as a telephone pole.

Caleb is hot enough the way he is, but now seeing this side of him, makes him hotter than hot. Basically, he's a fucking, blazing inferno in her mind! Her mind starts to daydream and fantasize about getting spanked by him. After a few seconds, she snaps out of it, and gives Caleb an amazing compliment.

"Caleb, I can't believe that a couple of days ago you knew nothing about spanking. It wasn't even on your radar, until you saw me spank my son, Dillon... And now, it's awakened a whole other side of you. A side that's so strong and so sexy, that it's going to drive women crazy! Trust me… I know from experience! And what impressed me the most was that you didn't hide anything. You have been totally honest with me and even bold enough to ask me to spank you the way I spanked my son. Now that I'm seeing this video, you even took it a step further. You dominated, spanked, and totally controlled your girlfriend like a true master. I'm beyond impressed. You're a natural spanker!"… Maybe we do need to go into business together!"

Caleb smiles from ear to ear, hearing her compliments. His dick remains pointing completely north, especially watching the video of last night's action. He replies back to Mrs. Doyle.

"Thank you for the compliment, Ma'am, but since I like to be spanked as much as I like to spank, I would say that makes me a natural switch."

"Yes it does, honey. You're totally correct about that. I'm going to share something with you that I never shared with anyone else… and I mean, no one else knows this." She tells him.

"About three years ago I was super frustrated with James. I mean, yes, I love him, but I needed more, sexually. I craved to be handled rough, spanked, dominated, and all those things. Unfortunately, he doesn't have it in him. It's just not who he is. So, I needed to satisfy this sexual need or I felt like I would live to regret it. So I actually hired a professional Dom. I wanted to fulfill a fantasy that I had."

"So what happened? Was it an amazing experience?" Caleb excitedly asks and waits for her response.

"It totally sucked! He was awful and I ended up walking out. First of all, he looked nothing like the pictures he sent me. That alone wouldn't have stopped me, because just about everyone always posts their best pictures, complete with filters that flatter, and software tricks. It was that he lacked creativity, effort, and didn't take control at all. Anyone can swing a strap or a riding crop and call themselves a Dom, but I wanted the mindset to go along with it… I knew what I wanted and I was willing to pay for it. I even created a scenario. So, when I showed up, it was obvious that he didn't put any effort into it. He didn't dress to the part, and there were no props at all. Basically, he did nothing to enhance or feed off my creativity... Fucking loser!"

"So what was the scenario that you wanted?" Caleb asks her.

Megan Doyle takes a deep breath and really reveals her soul to him.

"It was simple." Mrs. Doyle replies, "I just wanted an old-fashioned school scenario... Where the teachers were strict and didn't hesitate to discipline students. I gave him the choice to be the school principal, a professor, a teacher, school security, and I wanted to be the smart mouth, wayward student... It's not that hard, but I expected some effort. He didn't pick any of those... the jerk he was just dressed in leather pants, leather boots, looking like a motorcycle rider, carrying a riding crop... That wasn't what I had in mind. I was very clear and I wanted a school scenario, where I was the misbehaving student. My fantasy was to recreate some of those old school days, college, high school, with some extra kinks and added benefits... That's not rocket science!"

"That scene could've been so hot," Caleb replies. "I could absolutely picture you as a smart ass student."

She laughs, "Haha, yeah... it's too bad because I went all out. I dressed the part and had everything planned. I hid objects on me that could have gotten me in even more trouble. I had cheat sheets under my sleeves, wrote answers to tests on my arm, even hid some kinky things in my backpack... I put some effort in and did my part."

She continues, "I wanted so badly to get my plump ass tanned good, and I also wanted to struggle, and resist. I didn't want to just submit and get tied up with no effort. As hot as that is, it wasn't my fantasy. I wanted to be handled roughly... with force. I'm feisty, and I wasn't just going to take a spanking. He needed to handle me the way you handled Sarah. The way you got aggressive, forcefully pulled her over your knee, secured her arms, and prevented her legs from kicking... that was so perfect! And so fucking hot!"

Mrs. Doyle gasps as it's obvious that she's turned on thinking about that scenario. Caleb notices this and his dick is literally pulsating. It's dying for attention as he remains totally naked, sitting on her exam table. He can totally picture manhandling Mrs. Doyle, and going to town on her beautiful, round, pumpkin-shaped ass.

Mrs. Doyle's eyes continue to look Caleb's hot body up and down. She constantly pauses to stare at his penis before going back to look him in the eyes. Of course, Caleb, notices this and loves every minute of it. He's at that point once again, where he's about to make a move on her.

Mrs. Doyle's big, blue eyes looked down again at Caleb's erection. Once again, she fans her face with her hand to show him that she's overheating.

"Phew! Show me the part of that video where you get really aggressive with Sarah again!" She smirks.

Chapter 32

Caleb smiles back at her, then he navigates back to the part of last night's video where Sarah removes her blindfold and blatantly disobeys his commands.

"This is where I untied her, but I left the handcuffs and blindfold on her. There was no way I wanted to risk her seeing the marks on my butt from the spanking you gave me." He explained his reasoning to Mrs. Doyle to go along with his play-by-play of the video.

Just as he said, the video shows him untie Sarah's legs and arms, but he leaves the handcuffs and blindfold on her. Mrs. Doyle hears Sarah beg for Caleb's dick on the video.

"I want that dick, baby! Take these off... Let me touch you, suck you, fuck you!"

"Wow, she's really turned on and begging for you, Caleb." Mrs. Doyle comments as the video keeps playing.

"Oh, you're gonna get it, but tonight it's my way. The blindfold and handcuffs are staying on!"
Caleb replies back in a stern voice, then grabs Sarah, and walks her over in the direction of his sofa.

"Watch this part... This is where it gets really good!" Caleb excitedly tells Mrs. Doyle.

The video now shows Sarah being defiant and giving him attitude.

"I want to see you and touch you!" Sarah yells out as she reaches her hand downward to feel for his dick.

In the video, Caleb allows Sarah's hand to grab him, and feel his huge hard-on through his jeans. He then unbuttons and pulls his jeans together with his underwear down, slightly below his butt.

"And there's that amazing ass of yours!" Mrs. Doyle comments, "It sure is a thing of beauty... And Wow!... Look at those marks! It's a good thing she's blindfolded. I really went to town with my strap on that hiney of yours!"

"Yep, you sure did! That's why I needed to keep her blindfolded!" Caleb confirmed.

The video then shows Caleb taking Sarah's hand and placing it on his testicles, before guiding it upward to let her feel the full extent of his erection.

"There... You felt it!" He replies to Sarah, "Happy now?"

"Hell NO!" Sarah responds with more attitude as she drops to her knees and guides her tongue along the shaft of his dick.

Mrs. Doyle watches the video intently as Sarah's handcuffed hands are clenched to Caleb's testicles. She then opens her mouth and totally engulfs him. It then shows Sarah disobeying Caleb, and moving her hands upward to take off her blindfold.

Caleb comments on the video to Mrs. Doyle, "This is when I get really strict!"

Caleb turns the volume of his phone all the way up to make sure Mrs. Doyle hears every word.

"I told you this blindfold stays on!" Caleb sternly scolds Sarah in the video as he pulls away, and places the blindfold back over her eyes. He then reaches down and takes the long rope that was tied around the leg of the end table and wraps it to secure her arms around her waist.

"PERFECT!" Mrs. Doyle comments with excitement.

"So, you really want to be a bad girl and disobey me tonight?" Caleb responds on video, "Fine, I'll show you exactly how I handle bad girls!"

"God! You scolded her perfectly!" Mrs. Doyle compliments him again.

The video then shows Caleb pulling his pants and underwear back up and quickly sitting on the sofa. Without wasting another second, he forcefully pulls Sarah over his lap. He places his right leg over her legs to prevent her from kicking and raising her legs. He raises his hand high and delivers a flurry of relentless slaps to her ass.

The video has every once of Mrs. Doyle's attention as she sees and hears the loud slaps.

<SLAP><SLAP><SLAP><SLAP>

"OUCH! Okay, I'm sorry baby… Oow!" Sarah is desperately pleading.

After receiving a good spanking over his knee, Caleb then pulls Sarah off his lap and onto her feet. With an incredibly stern look on his face, he forcefully marches her to the sofa. Mrs. Doyle smiles as she watches the way Caleb manhandles his girlfriend into a position of lying flat on her back. Her arms are still bound to her waist, which makes Mrs. Doyle once again comment.

"I love this! You didn't let up, Caleb." She smirks and smiles at him before directing her eyes back to the phone screen.

Her eyes continued to be glued to watching the video. Mrs. Doyle takes in the way Caleb grabs a hold of Sarah's ankles and lifts her legs up into the diaper position. He then firmly tucks them under his left armpit and gives her body a little twist, to automatically make the sit spot region of her ass even more accessible.

This makes Mrs. Doyle comment, "Phew! I love the way you're manhandling her… So hot!"

The video plays and shows Caleb raising his strong hand and administering a serious spanking to Sarah in this diaper position.

<SLAP><SLAP><SLAP><SLAP><SLAP>

"OOOW!… OUCH!… OOOH!" Sarah instantly cries out.

"I told you, tonight it's my way!" Caleb scolds her as his hand rains
down with the utmost of intensity on her ass.

<SLAP><SLAP><SLAP><SLAP>

"YEOW!... I'm Sorry babe!… OUCH! Sarah's loud cries in the
video have Mrs. Doyle's panties completely saturated.

She continues to watch as Caleb doesn't hold back. He really
delivers a serious spanking, making sure every last inch of Sarah's
beautiful ass and upper legs are completely covered with his red
hand prints.

<SLAP><SLAP><SLAP><SLAP>
<SLAP><SLAP><SLAP>

"Oow!… I'm sorry!… Red!" Sarah yelled out her safe word.

"Oh My God!… That's hot, Caleb!" Mrs. Doyle tells him.

"Yep, that's when she used her safe word." He smiled at Mrs. Doyle.

Caleb taps the screen of his phone and turns the video off.

"Hey!… Don't you dare turn that video off yet. I want to see it to the
end! Mrs. Doyle commands.

Chapter 33

Caleb taps his cell phone and the video continues to play. It shows him instantly stop spanking Sarah since she just used her safe word. He then releases her legs from his hold, and pulls her up with haste. He still has that look of sternness and intensity on his face as he forcefully pushes her over the arm of the sofa. His strong left arm holds her in place as she's bent over with her beautiful, marked ass up high in the air. Caleb then quickly unbuttons his jeans and lowers them back down below his butt as he rams his dick with maximum force into her pussy.

"HOLY!" Mrs. Doyle blurts out as she watches the video.

Caleb continues to thrust and fuck her with force as Sarah goes into some heavy breathing, and lets out some incredibly sexy moans. He then grabs a handful of her long, brown hair and holds onto it like he's riding a horse as he continues to fuck her brains out with all the intensity he has. Sarah's moans of pleasure are getting to Mrs. Doyle as she is now totally craving to feel Caleb's dick inside her wet pussy more than ever.

"Oooo!… Yes!... Oh God!… Yes!… Mmmmm! Fuck me, baby… Harder!…" Sarah moans.

Mrs. Doyle's vagina is flowing like a raging stream into her panties as she watches the video of her young neighbor absolutely fuck the hell out of his girlfriend.

"I can't believe I'm watching a porno video of you… my young neighbor next door, who also happens to be my oldest son's good friend... Crazy!… But, it's so fucking hot! You're insanely hot, and Sarah's body is absolutely stunning!" Mrs. Doyle comments to him.

Caleb continues to ram every inch of Sarah's pussy with his huge dick. He gives one final tug on her hair accompanied by a few hard thrusts before he pulls out of her and cums all over her lower back.

"Good GOD! WOW! Just WOW!" Mrs. Doyle approves.

"It's not over yet." Caleb tells her with a smirk.

The video then shows Caleb grab a vibrator from his toy bag. He pulls Sarah up from the bent position over the sofa and once again lays her flat on her back. He spreads her legs and vigorously licks the wetness from the lips of her vagina.

"Mmmm!... Yes!... I'm gonna cum!" Sarah instantly called out.

Caleb turns the vibrator on and places it on the exact area of Sarah's clitoris that his lips are working on. Mrs. Doyle's eyes once again shine as bright as the sun watching Sarah wiggle her hips and slightly gyrate them to help navigate Caleb's lips exactly where she wants them.

The video plays and Caleb's continuing to let his tongue work its magic along with the vibrator all over the sensitive areas of Sarah's labia and clit. He then unties her arms, and removes the handcuffs from her wrists. Right away, Sarah instantly grabs the back of his head and holds him in place as she gyrates on his tongue, and she erupts into another orgasm.

"Yes!... Right there, baby!... Aaah!... YES!"

The video ends with Sarah's hot, young body shaking vigorously before calming down, when her climax is completely over.

"That's the end." Caleb tells Mrs. Doyle.

"That's got to be the hottest thing I've ever seen!" Mrs. Doyle replies.

Just as Caleb is about to get down from the exam table, Mrs. Doyle pushes him back down. She quickly slips her heels off, and then follows up and slides her wet panties off her legs as well. She grabs them and literally stuffs them into Caleb's mouth as she climbs up on the exam table and straddles him. She takes her right hand and grabs the shaft of his dick. Without wasting another second, she inserts it into her wet pussy.

"AHHH! YES!" She moans as she finally has Caleb's dick inside her.

She holds his hands in place over his head, signaling that she's the one in complete control. Caleb's tasting every drop of her moisture as her panties are stuffed tightly into his mouth. It feels amazing the way this beautiful, mature woman is riding his cock like a horse. He feels her thick but soft legs pressing against his body as she's fucking the hell out of him. His dick is also doing a number on her pussy and making her scream out like a banshee.

"Ahh! Yes! Oh my God! I wanted this… I needed this! I'm going to fuck you like you've never been fucked, Caleb!" Mrs. Doyle confidently announces.

As he experiences the way it feels to have her take complete control, it's one fuck that Caleb will never forget. To this point, he's basically banged the living daylights out of every young college girl around the area. This feeling and this experience with Mrs. Doyle is completely different as she takes control and shows him what a sophisticated woman is all about.

Her body is insatiable and her pussy feels like heaven to him. He's dying to rip her dress off and take in the view of her womanly physique. He wants to grab and slap her ass, and tries to free his arms from her grip, but she's not letting go of them. She holds onto them even tighter and keeps them pinned over his head.

"Don't even try to move, mister! I'm fucking you my way!" She tells him with that intense look on her face.

Megan Doyle is turned on more than she ever was in her 44 years of living. She grinds her curvy hips up and down on Caleb's dick as he lays beneath her. Although he loves the taste of having her wet panties in his mouth, Caleb's dying to kiss her and touch her. He can't, however, ignore the fact that he's enjoying the way she's riding his dick. He's literally getting the daylights fucked out of him and it feels insane! She's forcefully bouncing up and down on him, and pounding his dick with those wide, sexy hips of hers.

Caleb can't help but let out some muffled moans to compliment everything that he's feeling. Megan Doyle is letting out some moans of her own that let Caleb know she's enjoying every inch of him.

"Fuck! Yes! Ahh! Right there! Just like that!" She moans in ecstasy as she feels Caleb thrust his hips up.

"That feels so fucking good, sweetheart!" She compliments him as he syncs up his hip movement to hers.

Mrs. Doyle reaches out with one hand and removes her panties from Caleb's mouth. She keeps his arms held in place over his head, and creatively ties her panties in a knot around his wrists. Her right hand then grips his face as she opens her mouth and lets their tongues collide.

"Mmmmm!" Caleb quickly expresses the way her tongue feels and tastes.

He's kissed a lot of girls in his 22 years of living, but never a woman twice his age like Megan Doyle. Right now, the taste of her tongue, the softness of her full lips, and the way her hips are pounding him are sensations that are driving him wild. His girlfriend Sarah is just about as perfect and as sexy as a girl can be. She's almost 21, has the looks of a super model and the physique of a superhero goddess. Sex so far with her has been amazing, as the video confirmed, but right now Caleb can't deny the way he's feeling as Mrs. Doyle continues to fuck him with the intensity of a jack hammer.

"Mmm! Ooh!" Caleb moans from the force she's using.

He continues to enjoy the contrast of the soft, sexy way her tongue is sliding over his teeth and exploring every single inch of his mouth with the hard pounding of her hips as she rides him like a cowgirl. One thing is for sure, Megan Doyle is one sexy as fuck woman.

She's had this raging fire and all this passion locked away, deep inside herself for years, and she's finally exploding! Now, over the last few days, and ever since she first spanked Caleb, it seems that she's really come alive… And with a vengeance!

Mrs. Doyle's entire body is tingling in delight as her pussy is feeling every inch of Caleb's huge, young dick. Far too often, she's turned to her vibrator, which always does a great job. However, right now, the feeling she has going on in her vagina, coupled with the taste of his tongue, is lifting her up on cloud 9.

Chapter 34

"Oh my God, Caleb! You feel fucking insane! This dick of yours is amazing!" Mrs. Doyle compliments him through her heavy breathing, and in between their kisses, as she continues to fuck him senseless.

"Mmmm! I love the way you're fucking me! Ride me, baby! Fuck me harder!" Caleb continues to edge her on even more.
"Ride my dick!… Fuck me your way… Harder! Harder! I want every inch of that pussy!"

His dirty talk takes Mrs. Doyle to another level and a whole new high. It's definitely not something that she's used to hearing, especially from her boring, vanilla husband of 24 years.

"Ahh! Oooh!" Mrs. Doyle responds and grinds him even harder.

Caleb instantly replies.
"So, you like it when I talk dirty… In that case… I want every drop of that juice from your pussy... And just wait until I eat you out! I want you to sit on my face! I want to lick that pussy and continue all the way up to that luscious ass of yours! Then I'm going to rim you, bite your ass cheeks, and make you scream with pleasure."

His dirty talk has her in a total frenzy.

"Ahh! Yes!" Mrs. Doyle yells out, "Talk dirty to me!"

Caleb quickly and with ease, gives her a taste of the bad boy she's looking for and continues.

"I'll give you a reason to wash my mouth out with soap. I can't wait to fuck you my way! I'm going to bend you over and fuck you like you've never been fucked before! I will fuck you in every position imaginable. You think this is hot?… Just wait until I get at your pussy and fuck you my way! I will fuck you into oblivion!"

Mrs. Doyle is close to having a full-fledged orgasm as she continues to ride his cock. Caleb knows this and he doesn't stop. He continues to edge her on and talk dirty as they fuck with intensity.

"Then once I'm thoroughly done with your pussy, I'm gonna work that ass of yours inside and out! You wanna be a schoolgirl? Be a schoolgirl… I'll be your Principal… Principal Caleb!... I will chase you and forcefully strip you down to your birthday suit. You want a spanking? I'll give a spanking that you will never forget, Missy! I'll deliver my leather strap to your ass and I won't stop until you're crying a river! I will manhandle you, and pin you down just the way you crave. Then I'm gonna ram my huge dick up your beautiful, meaty ass! No one will handle your ass the way I will… You just wait until I get at it!"

That's all it took as Mrs. Doyle now clamps down on his cock and screams out, "Yes! I'm cumming! Aahhhhh!"

She grabs onto Caleb's face and gives him a kiss that's so sexy and filled with so much fire that it almost makes him cum as well. Being twenty-two years old definitely has its advantages, as Caleb can just about fuck all night without cumming… And even then, if he does cum, he can usually get hard all over again in a matter of minutes. Right now, his dick is still rock-hard as Mrs. Doyle's body relaxes and comes back down to earth. Caleb can't wait to strip her down and bend her over the exam table. As of now, he hasn't even caught a glimpse of that luscious body of hers.

Aside from her panties and heels, Mrs. Doyle remains straddled on him with every piece of her clothing still on. That pretty sundress flows over her hips as she embraces Caleb with another sexy kiss and warm hug.

"Hahaha… Phew! Wow! Oh, my God! That was amazing!" She tells him as she goes into a laughter filled with pure delight.

"This body of yours is insane, Caleb… It's been constantly on my mind from the moment I pulled down your pants and spanked your ass with my leather strap! Those cheeks of yours and this dick just drive me wild. And now, the way you just talked dirty to me… Blew my mind! I'll be ready for more, but first I'm gonna give you the blow job of your life! I can't wait to have your cock in my mouth!"

Caleb doesn't say a word as Mrs. Doyle's amazing tongue once again enters his mouth and gives him a steamy kiss. Her tongue feels so amazing in his mouth, that he knows he's about to experience euphoria when he feels it sucking his cock.

Mrs. Doyle ends her passionate kiss with a sexy bite on his lower lip. She gives him that little smirk of hers and says, "Now, it's time for me to get at that dick!"

She climbs off him and gets down from the exam table. She then extends her arm to guide Caleb to step off the exam table, and stand in front of her. The moment his feet touch the floor, she grabs a hold of his testicles with her right hand, and gives them a forceful little squeeze that makes him gasp.

"Cough!" She says in a stern, but very seductive voice, as she replays his exam, but now in a sexy way.

She then grabs the shaft of his dick with her left hand and shoves it fully into her mouth.

Mrs. Doyle goes to work sucking her young neighbors dick like it was the last one left on planet earth.
Caleb's head kicks back and his eyes close as he feels her tongue slide up and down, and then over the tip of his cock. He then feels the amazing sensation of her full lips tightening around the shaft of his cock as she forcefully sucks in. Once again, Mrs. Doyle, fondles his testicles as though she was examining them all over again. Her pretty fingers squeeze and hold each one individually with medium pressure before releasing and squeezing them again, adding a little bit more pressure each time.

Caleb lets out a sexy moan that confirms everything she's doing is driving him wild.
"Aahh! Fuck, that feels amazing! Mmmm! Ahh!"

Mrs. Doyle then cups both of his testicles in her right hand and squeezes them, as she digs the fingernails of her left hand into the fleshiest part of his right ass cheek.

Caleb's cheek feels the pain of her pinches at the same time his dick is experiencing the pleasure of her talented tongue. He's not just getting a blow... He's getting the mother of all blowjobs from his sexy, spanking neighbor. Megan Doyle is on fire, and unleashing every bit of pent-up sexual energy that she has on him. She's literally sucking him like a lollipop and savoring every inch of his dick.

Caleb looks down to take in the view of her going to town on his cock. He grabs a hold of her long brown hair, and continues to experience the pleasure of those full, strawberry lips of hers, wrapped around his penis. He then catches a glimpse of her pretty face, but is completely caught off guard as he sees tears flowing down like rain from her eyes.

He instantly backs away, putting a stop to his epic blowjob.

"Hey, what's going on?" He asks with a look of concern. Caleb reaches out his hand to pull her up from her knees, "Are you okay? What's up?"

Mrs. Doyle can't help it as the flood gates are now open. She stands up, looks him in the eyes, and lets it all out.

"I'm so sorry, honey. It's just that this is the first time I've ever cheated on my husband. Twenty-four years of marriage… twenty-fucking-four!… And, I've never taken it this far... I've thought about it in the past, even wanted to pay that Dom, as I've told you, but I never went forward until now. I'm just feeling really guilty."

She continues crying, "I'm doing exactly what I tell my kids not to do. I preach to them constantly, and I've even spanked Ryder for this very thing. Just ask him, I paddled his fanny until it was as red as an apple, when I found out that he cheated on his girlfriend! I always tell him, it's better to be honest and let them down easy. Tell them that you're not ready for a serious committed relationship, and that you want to casually date. And, don't even get me started on the topic of having unprotected sex! That's just unacceptable... And what did I do? I go ahead and shove your penis inside me without even thinking about a condom! That's just stupid of me!"

Caleb is feeling horrible and totally shell-shocked. Just a moment ago, he was lost in the clouds from the epic blowjob she was giving him, and now he's feeling like dirt. He embraces her with a warm, tender hug, and she continues to cry on his shoulder. Caleb has no idea what to say or how to respond. He's lost for words, just as he's lost his erection. At twenty-two years old, it's not really that big of a deal to him. He's cheated on just about every girlfriend he has been in a relationship with. He's also experienced being cheated on as well.

Mrs. Doyle regains her composure enough to apologize once again.

"I'm so sorry, Caleb. I didn't mean to bring you down. I guess I'm just a ball of emotions right now and all I can do is apologize to you."

Caleb replies, "It's okay. I understand. I'm not here to make things complicated for you. This is our secret and we never have to do any of this again. I appreciate and respect you more than you'll ever know. You are as beautiful on the inside as you are on the outside. You're such an amazing woman, a great friend, and a loving, dedicated mom. Everyone loves and admires you... including me. You have already changed my life, and made me not only realize, but also experience exactly what I've been missing. I will forget that."

Mrs. Doyle slightly pauses her cries after hearing those beautiful words from him.

"No, I don't want this to end. I really need this in my life. I'm just human and I guess my guilt has gotten the better of me at this moment. I'm thankful that it was you that I cheated, and did this with. You are sensitive, understanding, and way beyond your years. I want this relationship, and our agreement to continue. It's good for me. My body and my mind need this, and I think, at least I hope, that it's good for you as well."

Caleb quickly responds, "It's not just good for me... It's amazing and life-changing! It's the best thing that I've experienced... Ever! And I'm not talking about this sexual escapade that we just had... I'm talking about having structure, accountability, and someone like you in my life that will keep me in line. You shared with me how this resembled the relationship that you had with your college professor, so I know you understand everything that I'm saying and feeling. Yes, I admit that a large part of this is sexual, but it's much more than that. You and I also connect on an emotional level with honest and open conversations. We have the same mindset, and also the same fantasies."

Caleb chuckles and then continues.

So, how could it not be sexual? I mean, look at you... You're freaking beautiful and so damn sexy! Any guy, or girl for that matter, would want you to do the things that you do to me. You would have ass after ass waiting in line, and extending around the block, to get a spanking from you... And of course, I would be first in line!

Caleb's sincere words and that perfect touch of humor really resonated with her. She opens her mouth and kisses him with passion once again, then replies.

"I love the genuine trust and the bond that we've established so fast, honey. It's mind blowing that we can be this open and talk about anything, including our sexual fantasies and desires. I mean, you're half my age and you are so mature and beyond your years. You totally understand everything that I'm going through better than any guy my age would. I love having that trust and freedom to talk this way about sex, spankings, and sharing our fantasies."

Caleb jokes, "Yeah, I guess it's not everyday that a neighbor shares their porn video with you!"

Mrs. Doyle laughs and replies, "Haha... And what a video it was!... But honestly, I'm so sorry that I ruined the moment for you, sweetheart. Just so know, that dick of yours is exquisite! I loved having it in my mouth, as well as my vagina. I just need to take a breather and get my head back on straight. Maybe I'll try to meditate or just sleep on it. Let's touch base tomorrow and talk some more."

Caleb tries his best to comfort her, and say the right things, but he's obviously disappointed and clearly frustrated that she wants to end the night. He feels cheated, jipped, and even taken advantage of. After all, he didn't get his chance to do the things to her that he wanted to do. He tries to hide those feelings and replies.

"Look, I know you have a lot to lose, Mrs. Doyle. You have your husband, your kids, your house, your reputation... I get all of that... You can set the pace, on how, or if you want to even proceed. If this is too much and it's getting in the way of your life, we can just stop... plain and simple... No accountability, no spankings, no intimate conversations, and of course, no sex. You opened up a whole new world for me, and obviously for my girlfriend... that is, if her and I even stay together..."

Caleb's tone is now definitely showing some frustration, "I realize that it's all because of you that spankings will be a major part of my life. It might take me a while, but I'll be okay. Sooner or later I'll find another stern, no-nonsense woman that hares my kink. Someone who is into reddening my bottom when I need it... and vice-versa."

As much as he tried, those last few words didn't go over well with her. She's obviously way too emotional right now and her hormones are doing somersaults inside her body.

She gets that look of slight anger across her face, "Glad to know I'm so dispensable! Fine, go find yourself another woman to spank you... and so on... I'm sorry I got emotional and this breakdown happened.

I know you're disappointed, but like I said, I'm human! FUCK!.. just get dressed and let yourself out."

Mrs. Doyle storms out of the office area in her home and retreats to her bedroom, locking the door. Caleb gathers his clothing, gets dressed, and heads for the door. He hears the water running, which signals that Mrs. Doyle is most likely taking a bath to clear her head.

Caleb feels incredibly sorry for the words he just said, but he also feels incredibly frustrated as well. The fact is that Mrs. Doyle got what she wanted. Once again, she had Caleb in his birthday suit as she fondled him, fucked him like a jack rabbit, licked him like an ice cream cone, and got to experience an insane orgasm.

It's not that Caleb didn't enjoy all that, but he didn't get a chance to experience it from the same perspective. Not only did he lose his hard-on, but he didn't even get a glimpse at seeing that incredible body of hers. Sure, she fucked his brains, but she kept her sundress on, and got exactly what she wanted.

The more Caleb dwells on this, the more upset and frustrated he becomes. He so wanted to fuck her his way, and get a chance to do those dirty, kinky things he told her about. At least she could've finished that insane blow job and given him relief from that epic erection that he'd been sporting for hours.

Caleb, feeling a little heated, returns to his house and tries to cool off. He seeks refuge with a cold shower. It's really been one hell of a weekend to say the least.

Mrs. Doyle is also trying to relax herself down off the edge. She's in complete turmoil and is trying to find comfort in a warm bath. She's still trying to process everything that she's feeling for Caleb. She's feeling so much guilt, yet in some way, she needed to experience this. She'd been hiding these deep sexual desires and needs for way too long. She even tries to make an excuse and an argument for her actions and cheating on her husband. She talks to herself and says all kinds of things like…

"Jim's not into any of this kinky stuff… If I don't do it now while I still look good, then when?…
I've put myself and my needs aside for too long…
I'm more than just a mom… I'm a woman with desires and cravings… I do everything for everyone else, I need to do something for me…"

Her mind now proceeds to actually create dangerous images of a life with Caleb. The romance, the sex, vacations and traveling together… everything. She even pictures them living together in a full-fledged relationship. In this fantasy world there is no sign of her kids, her husband, the home she has now… nothing! Everything has changed.

Speaking of changes that are affecting many people's lives from this crazy roller coaster of a weekend, Sarah is more than ready for her mission. She arrives at Coach Miranda's condo, which is situated way across town. The young student can't wait to experience everything romantic and kinky with the sexy, sophisticated woman who coaches her baseball team. She's been hiding feelings for Coach Miranda for a couple of years now and this weekend finally made all that come to fruition.

Likewise for Miranda, who's about to be on the receiving end of everything that she's been craving and missing in her life. Just then, Sarah knocks on her door, and she excitedly opens it and lets her in.

The moment the door closes, they fall into a sexy, passionate, romantic kiss that could rival any movie scene. Once they come up for air, Sarah glances down at the large gym bag that she overstuffed with a number of sex toys, clothing, and a variety of implements. Without wasting another second, she pulls a blindfold out of her pocket, spins Miranda around, and quickly fastens it over her eyes. The next Miranda feels are handcuffs being slid onto her wrists as Sarah calls out in a more than sexy tone, "Tonight… You're all mine!"

Back on the other side of town, Caleb finally emerges from the shower. He's still quite heated and hasn't totally calmed down yet from everything that just went down with Mrs. Doyle. Regardless, he's ready to chill-out and call it a night. Just then, his cell phone rings. He answers to hear his good friend Christian's voice.

"Dude… Where are you? We're all here at the sports bar. We're supposed to celebrate your promotion. I have someone that is dying to meet you… Wait until you meet Bailey! You are going to flip the fuck out! She's hotter than hell and really wants to meet you… Get your ass down here!"

Caleb smirks then replies, "Okay bro, I could use a hot chick right now… give me 20 minutes… See ya' soon!"

Caleb gets himself together in record time and heads for his door. There is no doubt this weekend really has changed everything for so many people. It changed life as they knew it for Mrs Doyle, Caleb, Sarah, and now it's about to be the catalyst for Miranda, and possibly Bailey, as well.

He grabs his car keys and then pauses for a moment. His cute, sarcastic type of smirk said it all, as he then grabbed his gym bag full of toys and exited his house.

THE END

Thank you again for reading "The Weekend That Changed Everything". Your support means the world to me.

Please feel free to say hi and visit my website www.robinfairchild.com.

Also, please join my mailing list at robinfairchild_author@yahoo.com. You'll receive FREE books and substantial discount promotions as well.

As always, I sincerely appreciate any positive reviews and feedback that you can leave on this book.

Love and blessings,
Robin

Printed in Great Britain
by Amazon

29024457R00106